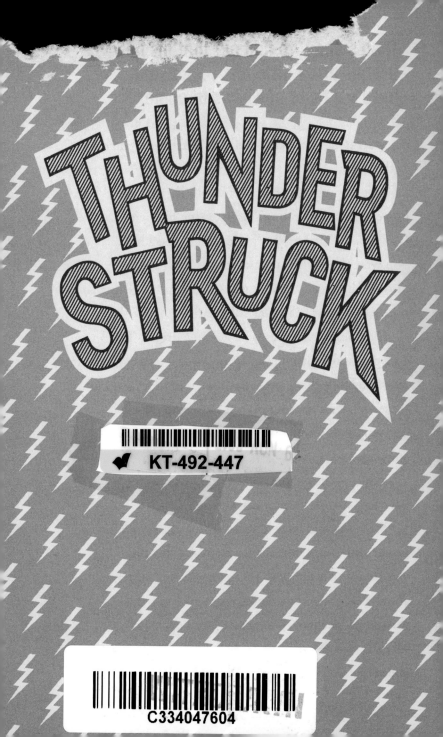

THUNDER STRUCK

KT-492-447

C334047604

Theo's about to find out that his new friends are a little bit . . . unusual. Here's a taste of what's to come!

Theo scratched his head, baffled. 'What were you doing at the hospital?'

'Just helping out,' said Lizzie, getting off the gravestone and stepping closer, eyeing him with fascination. 'That useless junior doctor decided you were dead when you weren't. I had to blow on her neck at about gale-force nine to get her to notice that your heart was still beating.'

Theo began to feel as if he was in a dream. This conversation kept slipping around in a weird way, making him struggle to hang on to the thread of it. One minute these kids were making perfect sense and the next, they might as well have just slipped into another language.

'Why . . .' he gulped, '. . . would you have to blow on a junior doctor's neck?'

'Well, I would have liked to smack her round the head,' said Lizzie, putting her hands on her hips. 'She was being such an idiot! There are loads of stories about kids going into shutdown . . . the heartbeat slowing to one or two a minute. It's a primeval survival trick. She should have known all about that. If I hadn't breathed on her and given her some goosebumps she might never have looked back at the monitor and you'd be a goner.'

'Lizzie . . .' Theo took a deep breath. 'What are you on about?'

'She couldn't smack her round the head,' explained Dougie, his voice slow and patient. 'Because we can't do that kind of thing. The only thing we can do is move air around a bit and make you feel colder. If we try really hard.'

'It's one of the worst things about being a ghost,' said Lizzie. 'There are days when I want to slap someone so badly I just . . . evaporate!' She went a little transparent as she said this.

Theo's mind sent a message directly to his legs. For a moment his knees went weak and began to buckle. And in another moment he was running along the main path through the graveyard, his breath coming hard and fast and his heart bouncing around inside his chest. He was shouting something in between his ragged breaths. 'NO!' (puff) 'NO!' (puff) 'IT'S NOT . . .' (puff) 'REAL!'

Back on the path Dougie and Lizzie stood side by side, watching him.

'Well, that went well,' said Dougie.

For Douglas Lane, wherever you may be

OXFORD
UNIVERSITY PRESS

Great Clarendon Street, Oxford OX2 6DP
Oxford University Press is a department of the University of Oxford.
It furthers the University's objective of excellence in research, scholarship,
and education by publishing worldwide. Oxford is a registered trade mark
of Oxford University Press in the UK and in certain other countries

Copyright © Ali Sparkes 2017

The moral rights of the author have been asserted

Database right Oxford University Press (maker)

First published 2017

British Library Cataloguing in Publication Data

Data available

ISBN: 978-0-19-2739360

1 3 5 7 9 10 8 6 4 2

Printed in Great Britain

Paper used in the production of this book is a natural,
recyclable product made from wood grown in sustainable forests.
The manufacturing process conforms to the environmental
regulations of the country of origin.

THUNDER STRUCK

Ali Sparkes

OXFORD
UNIVERSITY PRESS

CHAPTER ONE

'OK—let's get the first thing out of the way. Yes, yes—I'm called Theo. Go on. Have a laugh.'

Alisha was puzzled. 'Erm—OK. Ha ha . . .' She shrugged. 'But what's so funny about Theo for a name?'

The new boy puffed up his cheeks and blew out some air. 'Well . . . OK. Maybe Theo is OK, but TheoDORE?'

Alisha nodded. 'Well, yeah—I suppose Theo-DORE is a bit unusual. But there are worse names. You could be called Egbert. Or Tarquin,' she added. 'Or Bob. Bob Allhat.'

'Named after Theodore Roosevelt,' went on Theo, scratching at his shock of light brown hair and sitting down under the tree, as if she hadn't even said anything. 'I think me mam expects me to be president one day.'

'Well . . . you'd have to move to America first,' observed Alisha, also sitting down under the tree, but not too close. After all, this Theo was new and she had no idea what he was really like. 'Anyway, nobody's going to make a big deal about your name if you don't *tell* them it's TheoDORE and that your mum thinks you'll be president one day.'

'That's a good point,' said Theo. 'Happen I won't then.'

But Alisha could see Theo was probably going to get laughed at anyway. He was gawky, quirky and had that funny northern accent. He just attracted attention. The wrong kind. Alisha knew all about the wrong kind. It was the reason she was sitting here, under this tree . . . kind of hiding.

Far down the common, under a low grey sky, everyone else in her year was doing sports day practice. Normally they would be on the school field but a big new library extension was being built on part of it, so everyone had trooped over to the common instead. It was hot even though the cloud had rolled in. The parents were due any time now and Alisha was really, *really* hoping her mum and dad wouldn't show up. They always had to cheer *so loudly* and shout out her name and wave like a pair of demented gibbons. This made all the other kids nearly wet their pants laughing because she was, without doubt, the WORST at sport, out of every other kid in school. The waving and cheering usually happened just as she was shuffling in last in the egg-and-spoon race, with yolk dripping through her fingers and eggshell in her hair. Alisha sighed. She couldn't help it. She was short and dumpy and had all the speed and grace of a tipped-over tortoise.

'Maybe they won't come,' she muttered, quietly, hardly aware of Theodore now climbing the tree overhead.

'Maybe *who* won't come?' he yelled down, cheerfully.

'Nobody,' said Alisha.

'Maybe Nobody won't come?!' he squawked and when she looked up he was dangling upside down off a branch, his hair all stuck out and his face turning pink. He looked like a toilet brush. 'Funny name . . . Nobody.'

'Not as funny as Theodore,' she snapped. 'Mr President . . .'

'Oh look—don't *you* start!' he wailed. 'They'll all be at it!'

'I hate sports day,' said Alisha. 'I'm rubbish at every single bit of it.'

There was a flickering in the sky.

'It's proper puthery today,' said Theo.

'Proper *what*?' said Alisha.

'Puthery—you know—muggy. Thundery. We might get rained off. Shame though—'cos I'm brilliant at sports, me. I'm going to win the hurdles. It's all the other stuff I can't do. Can't do geography. Can't remember dates in history. Can't hardly add up, me.'

There was a flash. A big one. Down among the posts and hurdles a few of the kids screamed. Suddenly, big round drops of rain were pattering on the grass and splatting against the leaves and a rumble of thunder rolled around the valley.

'Yesss!' said Alisha, punching the air. 'Rain! Rain! Rain!'

'We should get back over there,' said Theo, sitting up on the branch of the oak. 'It's not safe here.'

'It's dry here!' argued Alisha. 'Look at them— they're getting soaked.'

'Yeah, but, didn't you see the gravestone?'

'You what?' Alisha peered up at the new boy, screwing up her eyes as another brilliant white flash hit the valley.

'The one in the cemetery!' he insisted, nodding towards the distant dark yew trees at the edge of the common.

'Oh yes! A *gravestone* . . . in the *cemetery*!' said Alisha. 'Whoever would have thought it?!'

'The one right by the entrance,' he went on, as if he was making sense. 'About those kids who got killed in the seventies. They were sheltering under a tree, right here on the common, when—'

But Alisha never got to hear what happened next. At that moment a brilliant pink-white light seared across her eyes and there was an amazing crack. Her body convulsed and lay still. Next to her, America's future president hit the grass like a bag of wet cement.

CHAPTER TWO

'What do you think? Are they coming over?'

It was a boy's voice. An older boy, thought Theo, dimly aware that he couldn't move and that there seemed to be a large lump of concrete on his chest.

'Not sure,' said a girl. Also older. Maybe fourteen or fifteen. 'Blow a bit of rain over this way, will you? I think her plaits are smouldering.'

'Ba-fa-ga,' said someone nearby. Theo thought it was probably that clever, wordy girl—Alisha. Didn't sound too clever now, though.

There was a sudden gust and the rain drove itself hard into the ground next to him. He could smell something scorched. Burnt.

'People coming now,' said the boy, whoever he was.

'Good,' said the girl. 'They might make it then. Although, in a way . . .'

'I know,' laughed the boy. 'They'd be fun, wouldn't they?'

'Selfish to think of it, though,' said the girl, closer to Theo now.

At last Theo managed to peel his lids off his eyeballs. The girl looked dim; shadowy. She had brown hair and a soft, kind smile. She was also a bit see-through.

'Doug!' gasped the girl. 'I think he can see me!'

Another head came into view, leaning in above the girl's. It wore a friendly lopsided grin and a floppy blond fringe. '*Oh* yes,' said Doug. 'Hello!' He gave a little wave. 'It won't last, Lizzie,' he told the girl. 'It's just a near death thing, you know. He'll forget.'

'Ah well,' sighed the girl. 'Cheerio then, Theodore. Nice meeting you.'

Theo blinked and they were gone. To be replaced by a man in a bright yellow jacket shoving a plastic mask over his face. 'Hang in there, son,' said the man. 'We'll sort you out!'

Groggily, Theo turned his head sideways and saw Alisha being carried off on a stretcher. Her shoes were gone and her socks were smoking.

Great first week at school, he thought, before passing out.

CHAPTER THREE

She could hear sniffing and gulping. There were beeping noises and a white light. And everything smelt weird.

'Where am I?'

'Alisha! You're awake! Oh thank god!' Suddenly Mum was all over her in an avalanche of blouse and cheek and familiarity. 'How are you feeling, sweetheart? How are you?'

'Come on, love—don't crowd her. Let her breathe!' came Dad's voice from somewhere behind. 'Alisha—you're in hospital. Do you remember what happened?'

She got up on her elbows and looked around, astonished. She *was* in a hospital; in a small room off the main ward. The walls were white and the bed was high and firm. There was some kind of monitor attached to her and a tube thing going into the back of her hand. Mum and Dad sat on either side of the bed, staring at her if she was a recently landed alien.

'What . . . happened?' She furrowed her brow and tried to remember. Where had she been? The last thing she remembered was the school sports day . . . the dread of having to take part and bear her parents' undentable enthusiasm as she failed miserably in every event. The rain on the leaves of the tree. That weird, hyperactive boy . . . Theo? Theodore! The future American president . . . and then . . .

'Pink light,' she said, aloud. 'There was an incredible flash.

Mum made a noise which was half giggle and half sob. Her face was puffy with crying and Alisha felt a stab of guilt. Had she done something to upset her?

'Baby . . . you were struck . . . by lightning,' breathed Mum, stroking her hair.

'But you're OK,' added Dad, hastily. 'It's incredible . . . but you are. You're OK . . . aren't you?'

Alisha slowly sat up. Was she OK? She felt strange . . . but not in any pain, except, now that she moved them, the soles of her feet.

'My feet are a bit sore,' she said, wincing.

'Yes! That was where the exit point was,' explained Dad. 'The lightning hit the tree and then branched out and got you. The doctor says it travelled down your left side, arcing across your heart, and then shooting down through your legs and out of your feet into earth. Your heart stopped for a little while . . . but there were medics on the field for the sports day and they got to you both in about forty-five seconds, they say.'

'It's a miracle you survived,' added Mum and then she just gave up the fight and burst into noisy tears.

'Both? Both of us?' Alisha called across the sobs. She patted Mum's shoulder as comfortingly as a recently electrocuted eleven-year-old could.

'Ah yes,' said Dad. He looked grave. 'There was a boy with you. He wasn't so lucky.'

'Time of death?' asked the junior doctor, wiping her hair out of her eyes with a weary sigh.

'He's not dead,' said Lizzie. 'Honestly—these junior doctors. Look—look at the monitor, you prannet!'

Theo did *appear* dead, to be fair. He looked quite seriously deceased. His face was chalky pale and a little blue around the lips and there was no obvious rise and fall in the chest. But that didn't mean he *was* dead and Lizzie was in a position to know.

'Twelve thirty-eight,' sighed the junior doctor, shaking her head. 'Poor kid. Can't have known much about it.'

'He's NOT DEAD, you dozy—'

'Blow on the back of her neck, Liz,' said Doug. 'Spook her a bit. Make her look again.'

For on the monitor there *was* a tiny peak on the flatline—the faintest beat—blink and you'd miss it. It even made a beep, but in the hustle and bustle of the noisy A&E department perhaps the resuscitation team couldn't hear that. Theo was in a state of shutdown but not death. Not yet.

Lizzie blew hard on the back of the junior doctor's neck. Goosebumps rose on it immediately and the young woman shivered and then briskly rubbed her shoulders. She turned around and stared at Theo.

'Here comes another one . . . look! LOOK at the monitor!' yelled Lizzie, right in her ear.

The doctor looked. Just as the tiny blip snagged through the flat white line on the screen.

'Hang on,' she said. 'We're not quite done here . . .'

'Well done!' said Lizzie as they got the defibrillator paddles out again and gave the poor boy another small dose of what Mother Nature had already walloped him with today.

'CLEAR!' yelled the doctor and Theo jerked on the trolley.

And then opened his eyes and shouted, 'SMOKING SOCKS!'

'He's brilliant,' giggled Lizzie. 'Can we keep him?'

'He's not ours,' sighed Doug. 'Give him back. He's still in the land of the living.'

'Hmmm,' said Lizzie, as they left the room. 'So why was he smiling at me?'

'He wasn't,' said Doug.

'Oh, he was,' she said. She turned to look into Doug's wide hazel eyes and he looked back at her, gnawing on his lower lip, not really ready to believe it. 'I think this is it,' she said. 'Finally. We've got one.'

'Good news!' said Dad, peering around the sideward door.

Alisha smiled back tightly, trying not to whimper. The nurse was dressing the weird, lightning-shaped burns on her feet. Every dab of the cool healing gel was making her gasp. There was a bit of the burnt lightning pattern on her left arm too, but it didn't sting so much.

'Wha-what's good news?' she squeaked.

'That boy who was with you,' said Dad. 'It was touch and go for a while but they managed to save him after all. He's going to be OK. Apart from the sore feet, that is. His socks were blown off too. And he's got some burns on his hands from the boiled sap which came out of the tree. Amazing!'

Alisha felt a weight lift off her. She had barely known Theo but the idea that such a bonkers, lively, annoying boy could suddenly be snapped out of life when she'd been spared, had been very hard to get her head around. She'd been stopping herself from thinking too much about it because every time she did, her heart started to do a little dance of panic in her chest. And as it had recently been struck by lightning this seemed a little dangerous.

Now it eased back into a regular rhythm and she felt a real smile crease her face for the first time since she'd regained consciousness. 'That's great,' she said. 'Is he awake?'

'Oh yes,' said Dad. 'Very awake! Talking non-stop and trying to walk on his bandaged feet. His mum's having to pin him to the bed!'

'That sounds like Theo,' said Alisha.

'So . . . is he a friend of yours?' asked Dad.

'Never met him until this morning,' said Alisha with a shrug. 'But I suppose you could say we've got something in common now.'

Dad chuckled. 'Hey—you'll never believe what Mum's doing right now.'

'What?'

'She's talking to a reporter! The local paper's all over this and the hospital public relations person said the BBC has been on the phone too. I think you and Theo are going to be famous.'

Alisha shuddered. She did *not* want her face plastered all over the news.

'Don't worry, love,' said Dad. 'No reporters or cameras will be showing up here.'

'Can I go home?' Alisha suddenly wanted her own bed very, very badly.

'Soon,' said Dad, gently mussing her hair.

'We just need to keep an eye on you overnight,' said the nurse, smiling and finishing the last of the bandaging. 'Make sure you're OK.'

'It's just that . . . I don't like being stared at,' said Alisha.

'Who's staring at you?' asked Dad, looking puzzled.

'They are!' Alisha waved towards the window in the side-ward door. An auburn-haired girl who looked about thirteen and a taller, older-looking boy with a floppy blond fringe, stood on the other side of it, grinning in at her. As Alisha pointed towards them the girl turned and punched the boy lightly on the arm with a triumphant look on her freckled face.

'Who?' asked Dad, sounding a little worried.

'That boy and girl, right there,' insisted Alisha. 'Staring! I call that rude.'

Dad and the nurse looked at the door and then at each other. The nurse said: 'I'll get the doctor.'

CHAPTER FOUR

'Theodore. Theodore Rooney,' said Theo, grinning like an idiot.

Alisha winced. She knew what was coming next.

'I'm named after Theodore Roosevelt,' he told the assembled reporters. 'I think my mam wants me to be president one day.' They laughed and several cameras flashed.

A slim, fair-haired lady ducked under a long pole, with a fluffy microphone on the end which looked like a mistreated guinea pig. 'So what can you remember about what happened?' asked the BBC correspondent.

'Well, I could see there was lightning in the sky,' said Theo, his dark-blue eyes sparkling. He clearly *loved* the attention. 'I said we needed to get away from the tree. Lightning strikes often happen on trees—you're not safe underneath one. Really you need to be face down on the grass as far from a tree as you can get. In fact—ideally—you need to have your head down and your bum up in the air, so if you get struck it goes straight down your legs and not through your heart.'

'Wow. You seem to know a lot about this!' said the BBC woman amid laughter from all the other media people.

'Well, I knew we should get away,' said Theo. 'But by the time I'd said it, the lightning had hit us. I don't remember much about it apart from wondering why Alisha's socks were on fire.'

The audience gasped and the cameraman zoomed straight on to Alisha's bandaged feet.

'How are the feet now, Alisha?' asked the BBC woman.

'Um, not too bad,' mumbled Alisha. Her head was heating up. She knew she was blushing scarlet. Oh *great.*

Just a nice little chat to someone from the papers is what mum had said. She hadn't mentioned the whole room full of cameras and journalists and lighting and sound booms. And then someone counting backwards and saying 'LIVE in five, four . . .' and then signalling the last three beats before—BANG—on *telly*! No running away, either. Not when your feet were pair of grilled burgers.

'The doctors think she'll be able to walk on them

again in about a week,' Mum was saying. 'And there'll be some interesting scarring on the soles for a while . . . a bit of a memento!'

'You must have been terrified when you heard the news,' said the BBC woman.

'I was in pieces,' said Mum, squeezing Alisha's hand. 'Poor Alisha had to comfort *me* when she woke up.'

The BBC woman turned to camera. 'With me is Dr Karish, who has been looking after Theo and Alisha since they were brought in to A&E on Monday. Dr Karish, what would you normally expect to see when a lightning strike survivor comes in?'

Dr Karish stepped up to the camera and Alisha sighed with relief that it was no longer focused on her.

'Alisha and Theo were very lucky,' said the doctor. The full force of the strike hit the tree and only part of it branched off and hit them—which means they got a lesser strike. Their hearts were stopped for a short while but, thanks to the medics who were on hand for the school sports day, they were resuscitated very quickly which means that their brains were never starved of oxygen—as you can tell from talking to Theo!'

'We certainly can!' chuckled BBC woman. 'Are there likely to be any after-effects?'

'It's hard to say,' said the doctor. 'It's a traumatic thing but children are very adaptable and tough. They bounce back. There's every reason to assume that Theo and Alisha will be fine.'

'Apart from the hallucinations,' muttered Alisha. Theo looked across at her and raised his eyebrows. She shook her head briskly and stared back down at her bandaged feet. She was certainly not going to tell him about *that*. When Dad and the nurse had both said there was nobody looking in at the window, even though she could see those two kids, plain as day, she'd started to get that panicky heart dance again. But by the time the nurse had opened the door to fetch the doctor there was nobody outside at all.

'It's not unusual for people's minds to play tricks with them after this kind of thing,' Dr Karish had told her after a quick check of her eyes (normal). 'Your brain is a very sensitive machine—and it's just had to deal with nature's version of an EMP bomb. You know? An electromagnetic pulse . . . ? The kind of thing terrorists are always threatening to unleash to wipe out all our technology?'

Alisha nodded. She knew about EMPs.

'So—it's not surprising that your brain's throwing a bit of a wobbler,' went on the doctor. 'Don't worry about it. You might get one or two other glitches in your software . . .' he tapped her on the head, 'over the next few hours, but it'll settle down soon.' He'd given her parents a reassuring smile. 'She's made of tough stuff!'

She didn't feel tough now, though. She just felt very, very embarrassed, sitting here with feet that looked like something from a pharaoh's burial chamber. When would this *end*? The lights were making her sweat.

At last the live broadcast did end. But no sooner had the BBC team switched off its lights than the newspaper and radio and website reporters gathered around to ask all the same questions again. And then she had to pose for pictures with Theo, close together like they were best mates. Theo didn't seem to mind but Alisha cringed. She would never hear the last of this at school. Never.

Finally the PR woman from the hospital stepped in and said the patients were getting tired and that was enough—and Alisha and Theo were at last wheeled back to the children's ward. Their mums and Alisha's dad walked a little way behind, chatting to each other—sharing their relief. And for a minute or two, Theo was quiet. The porters wheeling them along were quiet too, as if they knew that any more chirpy questions would be too much.

Theo glanced across at Alisha as his wheelchair kept pacc. 'What did you mean . . . about hallucinations?'

'Nothing,' she said.

'No—you said it. I heard you. What did you mean?'

'It's *nothing*,' she said, feeling irritable and tired. 'I just thought I saw some things that weren't there. Dr Karish says it's just the brain kind of . . . rebooting.'

Theo said nothing. And that was pretty weird.

CHAPTER FIVE

The first day back at school was exciting. Everyone crowded around Theo in the playground, demanding to hear the story over and over again—and look at his feet. He'd taken his socks and shoes off and put them back on again at least ten times before the first bell. Everyone was so amazed at the lightning pattern scars and the fading blisters on his palms.

In class Mr Carter showed him all the stuff they'd been doing for a special weather project in honour of the school's famous lightning strike survivors. There were loads of paintings and posters and diagrams—even poems—all around the walls. And someone had made a huge lightning bolt out of metres of tin foil and hung it across the classroom ceiling.

All the newspaper cuttings were up in the corridor, along with pictures of Alisha and him on the TV and quotes from what they'd said. Mostly his quotes. Alisha hadn't said much. There was even a letter to them both from the local TV station weather presenter! It was in pride of place in the centre of the display.

But by lunchtime, as he headed into the dinner hall with his feet stinging in his shoes, Theo realized the novelty was wearing off. It was actually pretty tiring having to keep telling his story, and the soreness on his soles was also sapping his energy; something almost unheard of for Theo. And then Alisha arrived, looking as wiped-out as he felt, and for the first time he felt a real pang of sympathy for her. He knew exactly how she felt. He got some fish fingers and beans and went to sit next to her at the corner table.

Alisha rolled her eyes when she saw Theo heading for her. 'Oh no,' she groaned. 'Seriously?!'

'It's a bit weird isn't it?' said Theo. 'They won't leave me alone!'

Alisha glanced around the room and spotted several girls in her class giggling together and glancing over at them. It had begun. 'Look—it'll only get worse if we sit together,' she hissed.

'Why? What's up with that?' he asked.

'You *know* what I mean! They just won't shut up about it. We'll be the Lightning Twins! Or the Thunder Couple. Or something even more lame than that.'

'Who cares?' he said, throwing a chip up into the

air and then catching it in his mouth. 'Don't bother about them!'

Alisha sighed and closed her eyes. She *did* bother. That was the problem.

Kirsty Fellows wandered up to them, while the rest of her group watched in delighted anticipation. Kirsty was tall and blonde and great at sports. A popular girl. One of the girls who groaned and protested if she ever got saddled with dumpy, useless Alisha on the netball team. 'Hey, Alisha—Theo,' she called out as she reached them. 'When you two met was it—like—electric?!'

Theo guffawed and Alisha winced. 'Yeah! It was a bolt from the blue!' Theo said.

All the girls shrieked with laughter.

Alisha got up and hobbled towards the dining room door. She had to get away. Even if it felt like walking on hot coals.

And it did.

By the time three fifteen came around, Theo was glad to get away from school. He'd only been there for one week before the lightning strike and hadn't made any friends. The other boys had made fun of his accent and kept saying things like, *Oh 'eck as like! It's that lad from oop north!* and other stupid stuff.

He hadn't minded all that much. He knew he'd make a friend sooner or later. He was aware that he was hyper and annoying to some people, but he could also make other kids laugh and that's what usually got him through.

But no need. Now he was Thunder Theo with an instant bunch of mates. Kind of. He wasn't sure how many of them he actually *liked* yet, but it was nice to have kids interested in hanging out with him. He just wondered how many of them would still be saying hi to him in the corridor once they'd got over all the excitement.

Theo walked home slowly, rolling his feet from heel to toe, trying to ease the soreness. If he walked too fast or stomped too hard the stinging was enough to make his face screw up. He glanced across to the soft green grass of the verge. It led away up the road and then there was a left hand turn into the common. His house was further along on the right but the way there was all pavement. He could loop around through the common and join the path further down, quite close to his house. It was a longcut rather than a shortcut, but a much more comfortable journey. Also . . . he wanted to see the common again. The tree. He wanted to look at where it had happened.

He ambled along the verge and then turned left. The tree was at the top end of the common and would make his journey home even longer, yet he couldn't resist. He struck out across the wide expanse of springy turf. It rose gently towards a boating lake which was surrounded by a raised oval concrete pathway, halfway up the common. Not far beyond that was the top field where the sports day had been taking place last week. And off to one side of that was the oak tree.

From a distance it looked much the same, but as he got within a few metres he could see a black line running down one side of the trunk. Above the line, amid the bright green foliage, a thin swathe of crispy brown leaves snaked down from the very top of the tree. The black line on the trunk was glistening and gave off a smell of burnt sap. Theo glanced at his palms where there were still a few pale blisters. He'd been burnt by boiling sap, Dr Karish had said.

He stepped closer and pressed his right palm to the dark line. The aromatic resin—like a scab across a wound—was set hard and knobbly.

'Looks like we both got off lightly,' he told the tree.

'You did,' said a girl from up in the branches. 'Not everyone does. Loads of people suffer memory loss, ringing in the ears, sleep disorders, dizziness . . . memory loss.' She giggled. 'But you seem OK!'

Theo took a sharp breath and stared up at her. She looked familiar.

'Hey . . . weren't you here last week? When I got struck?'

She nodded, beaming down at him. Her gingery-brown hair was parted down the middle, shoulder-length and flicky, like angels' wings on either side of her temples. She was wearing red shorts with a kind of bib thing attached to them and a mustard-yellow polo neck sweater. There were lots of badges on the bib and a long knotted necklace of tiny multicoloured beads swung around the polo neck. The sandals on her feet were beige and had thick wedged soles. And she was wearing them with white knee-high socks.

Theo wasn't exactly up to the minute with girls' fashion, but even *he* knew this was a pretty weird look for a girl this age—around thirteen or fourteen, he guessed.

'Yeah—I was here. I'm always around here. So is Dougie, although he's wandered off somewhere right now. How *are* you? No spasms?' She beamed cheerily at him.

'Um . . . no,' said Theo. 'I'm OK.' Although he *was* feeling a bit goosebumpy, if he was honest. There was something strange about the girl. He'd seen her somewhere else too. Where?

'How are your feet?' she asked, making a pendulous twirling circle with her beads. 'Still sore?'

'How do you know my feet are sore?' he asked, puzzled. She was too old to be at his school, where it was common knowledge.

'Well of *course* they're sore!' she said. 'You won't be disco dancing for a while, I bet.'

Theo realized she'd probably seen him on television. Everyone who'd seen it would know about his and Alisha's feet. THAT was it. No great mystery. So why did he still feel weird . . . ? 'No . . . probably not,' he said. 'But that's OK. Disco's not my thing.'

'Disco's *my* thing!' said the girl. 'Doug thinks it's stupid too but I've seen him do it when he thinks I'm not looking.' And she jumped down from the branch with a chitter of beads and began boogying about on the grass, left hand on left hip and right hand flicking back and forth from the left hip and up into the sky. 'Burn, baby, burn!' she sang. 'Disco infernooooo . . .'

He had to laugh. She looked completely bonkers.

'Geddit?' she grinned. Her eyes were bright blue and her face was dotted with small brown freckles.

'Burn, baby, burn!' Swaying her hips in her short-dungaree thingies, she jabbed her fingers repeatedly at him, still in her funky disco routine. 'Only a bit. You didn't get too crispy. Although you were nearly a goner there for a while, even so.'

'You're nuts!' he said, grinning back. 'Yeah . . . they told me I was nearly dead. I don't remember anything about it really. Except . . . *you*. You were leaning over me, weren't you? Just before the medic guy showed up.'

'Uh-huh. You should have seen your hair. All stuck up on end. You looked like a Gonk.'

Away in the distance an ice-cream van chimed out a jarring melody and some kids down by the boating lake started whooping with excitement.

Theo had some money in his pocket. He thought about a cornet with a chocolate flake in it. He wondered if the girl would want one too.

'Fancy an ice cream?' he asked.

She smiled at him and swung her beads around again, like a lasso. 'Nobody has asked me if I'd like an ice cream for *ages.*' She sighed and let the beads drop. 'I'd *love* one, Theo. But I can't have one. Thank you anyway.'

He shrugged. He eyed the ice-cream van where a small queue of kids was already forming in the late afternoon sun. 'OK . . . well . . . I'm going to get one.'

'Enjoy it!' she said. 'Have one for me!'

'OK, I will, er . . .' He realized she hadn't told him her name. 'What's your—?'

He didn't finish the question. As soon as he'd glanced back he was silenced by surprise. The girl was gone. He glanced around him, wondering if she had suddenly sprinted away, but saw nothing at all. She wasn't back up in the tree, either. Weird.

CHAPTER SIX

'Hey! Alisha! Wait!'

Alisha turned around as she reached the corner of her road. She saw Kirsty Fellows and her best friend, Sophie Clarke, running to catch up with her.

'We were going to offer to carry your stuff for you,' puffed Kirsty, as she caught up. 'But we didn't see you leave!'

Alisha smiled at them both, hoisting her book bag over her shoulder. 'It's OK. I'm all right,' she said.

'Must be painful, though,' said Kirsty. 'Are there still bandages on?'

'Yes, but only those stretchy ones like socks. They'll be off in a couple of days. It's not too bad,' said Alisha.

'So . . . what was it like, being on TV? It looked SO cool!' said Sophie. 'I would LOVE to be on BBC Breakfast. Was it amazing?'

It hadn't been amazing at all, thought Alisha. Just embarrassing and tiring. But she said: 'Yeah, it was really cool. There were all these lights and booms. You know—those furry microphones on poles. And cameramen and all that.'

'You didn't say much, though, did you?' said Kirsty. 'Thunder Theo did all the talking. He's weird, that one. Do you fancy him or what?'

'What?! NO! No I don't!' spluttered Alisha.

'But you were under the tree together!' giggled Kirsty. 'That's a bit romantic, isn't it?'

'*I* was under the tree! He just came along and started climbing it like some kind of hyperactive monkey,' said Alisha. 'I'd never said a word to him before!' *Argh!* Now she was blushing furiously again and saying too much. It made it look like she was denying something that was secretly true. How could she stop all this? 'Why?' she asked, suddenly. 'Do YOU fancy him?'

'Alisha,' said Kirsty, with mock gravity. 'We're not even in secondary school yet. I don't have time to think about boys! Honestly—you're obsessed!'

'But I didn't even *start* this!' squawked Alisha. 'You were the one—'

'Look, it's OK!' said Kirsty, patting her on the shoulder. 'We won't tell anyone. It's fine if you have a thing for Theo. It's perfectly all right.' Behind her, Sophie was convulsing with giggles. 'After all . . .

you both had an enormous shock. A near-death experience. You're bound to have a special bond now.'

Alisha felt a wave of frustration and panic. She stopped dead and dropped her bag on the floor. Turning to Kirsty and Sophie she took a deep breath and yelled, 'Listen! Theo is a complete lame brain and I wouldn't touch him with a BARGE POLE!'

Kirsty and Sophie bit their lips and widened their eyes. They weren't even looking at her. They were looking over her shoulder. Alisha spun around and saw a boy walking away from them. He'd just emerged from one of the cuts that led out of the common, holding a half-eaten ice-cream cone. Theo glanced back once and then just kept going. There was no possible way he had missed what she'd just bawled out.

Alisha grabbed her bag and ran off home to peals of laughter from Kirsty and Sophie. Even the blazing pain across her soles could not slow her down.

Next day at school, Theo did not sit with her at lunchtime. In fact, he didn't come anywhere near her. This was good, Alisha told herself. This was what she had wanted. There were a couple of girls from her class sitting with her. Talking to her. Normally nobody bothered to speak to her unless they wanted a bit of help with some homework or to ask some other favour. She was definitely *slightly more popular* now than she had been last week.

But, as she scooped up a forkful of baked beans, she felt bad. She really wished she hadn't shouted out at Kirsty and Sophie yesterday, right at the moment Theo showed up. Theo was OK, really. He didn't deserve to be called a lame brain. Suddenly she remembered something he'd said to her, just before the lightning strike. About being good at sports but . . .

'It's all the other stuff I can't do. Can't work out geography. Can't remember dates in history. Can't hardly add up, me.'

Oh no. He already thought he was rubbish at learning stuff. And she'd called him a lame brain. Alisha put down her fork and felt her insides crunch up. It was like when she ran around on the netball court, totally failing to ever catch the ball and never being in the right place at the right time. The other girls would shout out in frustration. 'CATCH! CATCH IT! *CATCH IT, ALISHA*! Aaaaw! She's USELESS!'

It wasn't fun being no good at something. And it was even less fun when people kept reminding you.

So that's what she had done yesterday. To Theo. And now she came to remember the conversation under the tree, she also recalled him warning her to get away because they were in danger. And he was right. So obviously he was cleverer than he thought he was.

'When you're on TV again,' Emma Franks was saying, her face lit up with excitement and her red hair flopping across her cheeks, 'can we come on with you too? As your friends. You know . . . talking about how great you were.'

'Yeah!' chimed in Rosie Willis. 'I could say *"She was so full of life!"* They always say that, don't they?'

'Erm . . .' said Alisha. 'I think that's what they say when someone's dead.'

'Well . . . you were *nearly* dead,' said Rosie, her pink round face alive with enthusiasm. 'So . . . you know . . . we could be talking about how relieved we were that you didn't die but that if you had, we'd have really missed you and all that.'

'Would you?' asked Alisha.

'Of course,' said Emma. 'It would be a tragedy. We'd all be putting flowers under that tree and sobbing and there'd be counsellors brought in to school to help us cope with the trauma.'

'They'd probably shut the school for a week,'

added Rosie, a wistful look in her small brown eyes. 'So we could all come to terms with the terrible loss. And we'd both be there, under the tree, all tearful, when the TV cameras came to film a poyn . . . a poyi . . . you know—'

'A poignant scene?' prompted Alisha, with one eyebrow up.

'Yeah! That's it!' said Rosie. 'A poy-nant scene! That means sad, doesn't it?'

'Tragic,' said Emma. 'So tragic.' She sighed and it actually looked as if she was welling up a bit.

'Well, I'm really sorry,' said Alisha, getting to her feet. 'But I *didn't* die, so you can't stand around for the cameras being tragic and poy-nant.' Both girls looked at her, wide-eyed, as if their feelings had been hurt. 'Maybe another time,' said Alisha with a tight smile. 'Hey—I might get a fatal infection in my feet! There's still hope!'

She stalked away with her head high. Although her feet still twinged too much for her to stalk successfully. It was more of a fast limp, and hampered by the fact that she had to carry her tray to the scraps bin and scrape her plate first. She heard Emma say: 'Honestly! Just because she got struck by lightning she really thinks she's *it*.'

Well that's great, she thought, dropping her knife

and fork into the cutlery bowl with a splosh of grey soapy water. *Just great. I find some new friends and they sit around, cheerfully wishing I was dead.*

She wanted to be popular—but not *that* badly.

A whole afternoon stretched ahead. She'd be stuck in class with Emma, Rosie, Kirsty and Sophie. All probably wishing she was dead. It wasn't *personal* but that didn't really make her feel much better.

Alisha wandered down the corridor past the coat pegs, towards the double doors to reception. A phone was ringing but nobody was answering. Beyond the double doors the afternoon was warm and sunny. She could go. Right now.

Alisha took a deep breath and glanced around her. The corridor was empty. She reached up to punch the DOOR RELEASE button on the wall. There was a buzz as the electronic lock disengaged and she pushed the door open. She walked through reception and then outside to the wrought iron gate. At any second she expected a shout from a passing teacher or dinner lady. But nobody saw her. Nobody tried to stop her. So she lifted the heavy latch on the gate, swung it open and stepped out on to the lane.

She had never misbehaved at school in her life.

Until now.

CHAPTER SEVEN

To the memory of

DOUGLAS CRANE

Aged 14 years

Son of Douglas and Renee

Killed by lightning on the common with his friend when sheltering from a storm on

28 JUNE 1976

SAFE WITH JESUS

The gravestone was a simple rectangle, set into the earth. It was grey and splodgy with green lichen. Theo felt his skin prickle in the cool shade as he read the words. He'd seen them several times before.

The cemetery was a shortcut from his house to the common and he'd spotted the stone, right by the path, on the first day he'd arrived with his mother, just three weeks ago. Having the common so close to their new house partly made up for all the friends he'd had to leave behind when Mam got her new job down south. He'd been through the cut, past the gravestone plenty of times—but although it was interesting and sad, he'd not really given it much thought until last Monday, just before the lightning hit the tree.

Now it seemed . . . well, a lot sadder and a lot scarier. He could picture his own name on that headstone, with different dates. And the friend would be Alisha. Although Alisha wasn't his friend. He sighed. She'd seemed OK, but after hearing her with those two girls from school yesterday, he guessed she was pretty much the same as most of the other girls he'd met since coming down south. Snooty and unkind.

OK, so he *might* be a lame brain, but she didn't have to shout about it, did she?

He crouched down and traced his fingers across the lettering on the headstone. 'Sorry you didn't make it, Douglas,' he said.

'It is sad, isn't it?' said someone behind him.

Theo jumped to his feet and turned around. A boy

was on the other side of the path. He was lounging on one of the large tomb-like graves with faded letters chiselled all around its sides. He was stretched out right across the top as if it was a cabin bed, propped up on one elbow.

'Um . . . yeah,' said Theo, embarrassed. 'Look . . . I don't normally talk to gravestones. It's just that . . .'

'You're the kid who got struck by lightning last week,' said the boy. He was cheerful-looking, with longish fair hair which flopped over his forehead. His clothes were . . . interesting. He wore flared brown trousers with pockets right down the legs and a stripy nylon shirt in clashing shades of brown, burgundy, and blue. The collar on it had long points. His shoes looked a bit like the cheap plimsolls Theo used to have for games lessons until he persuaded his mam to get him some proper trainers in Year 5.

'How are you?' the boy asked.

'Um . . . y'know—middlin',' said Theo. 'Feet still a bit sore, but getting better. My teeth hurt more, right now. I've just been to the dentist.'

'I guess metal fillings don't much like thousands of volts passing through them,' observed the boy. 'That's going to sting a bit, isn't it?'

'They were just feeling . . . tickly,' said Theo. 'Like an itch you can't scratch. The dentist made them worse. Are you from Vale Academy?' he added. The boy looked about fourteen or fifteen so he couldn't be at Beechwood Junior.

'Nah,' said the boy. 'Hill Farm Comprehensive.'

'Oh,' said Theo. The local secondary school here was called Vale Academy. Perhaps this Hill Farm place was a school outside this area. 'What's that like? Any good?'

'Haven't been for ages,' said the boy, sitting up and jumping down off the grave. 'It was all right the last time I was there.'

'Why haven't you been?' asked Theo. 'You been excluded?'

The boy laughed. 'You could say that!'

Theo felt the prickles on his skin again. Was this boy a 'troubled' boy . . . ? It seemed kind of dangerous and he quite liked that. He'd been friends with a boy who was always getting kicked out of schools back up in Rotherham. He'd been great company. Until he was sent away to a young offenders' institution for setting fire to something. Or someone.

'It's nice . . . you know,' the boy was saying. 'That you bothered to come and see the gravestone.'

'Oh . . . that,' Theo turned to look back at the headstone. 'Well . . . I feel a bit of a connection now. After . . . last week.'

'I'd say you've *definitely* got a connection,' said the boy with a smile that lit up his pale face. 'It's good to see you Theo. And even better that you see me.'

'Um . . . right. OK.' Theo found himself staring again. There were weird kids on this common. Maybe this boy knew that odd girl who was up the tree yesterday. 'So, do you come here a lot? With your mates? Will I see you about?'

'I've only got one mate—and she's a girl. Lizzie. But yeah—we're always hanging around the common.'

'Lizzie? Has she got gingery hair and freckles?' asked Theo, brightening with curiosity. 'Likes to climb trees?'

'Yeah, that's her. But who doesn't like to climb trees?' asked the boy, grinning and digging his hands into the deep pockets of his odd trousers.

'Well . . . no girls I know ever do,' said Theo. 'They're all too worried about messing up their designer jeans or dropping their phones or something.'

The boy looked baffled. 'That's just weird. Why would you take a telephone up a tree?'

'Search me,' shrugged Theo. 'If I had one there's no way I'd risk getting it all scratched on tree bark.'

The boy continued to look baffled. 'But . . . what about all the wires and . . .'

'Honestly, Dougie, you're such a freak!' came

an amused high voice behind Theo. 'He means MOBILE phones! Not the clunky thing on your mum and dad's hallway table!' Theo jumped and spun around to see Lizzie perched on the lightning strike boy's gravestone—her feet squarely (and rather disrespectfully) planted right across the grassy grave mound, still in their wedged sandals and white socks.

'Oh. Hello again!' said Theo.

'I knew that!' protested the boy. 'I was just . . . I forget sometimes.'

'Seriously, we've drained the batteries on enough iPhones and iPads over the years!' mocked Lizzie. She beamed at Theo and gave a little a wave. She looked *delighted* to see him. Really delighted. 'What did I tell you, Dougie? I told you he'd see us again!'

'Again . . . ?' Theo was feeling a bit disorientated.

'Don't mind him,' said Lizzie. 'He's just stuck in the past. *I'm* the one who moves with the times!'

Theo looked sceptically at her outfit. She had on exactly the same clothes as yesterday—the funny shorts/bib combo and the polo neck sweater and beads. She saw him peering at her clothes and looked herself up and down before glancing back up at him with a shrug. 'Well, OK, my outfit's a bit retro . . . but that's what's in right now. The seventies look!'

Dougie snorted with laughter. 'Yeah . . . it only took forty-odd years to come around again.'

'So . . .' Theo said. 'When did I see you before . . . Dougie? I don't remember.'

'We were both there when you and Alisha got struck by lightning,' said Lizzie. 'Don't you remember him? You remembered me.'

Theo thought for a moment. He *did* remember someone else with Lizzie under the tree. Just couldn't picture his face. 'So . . . did you see us actually get struck?' he asked, fascinated. 'What happened? Were we twitchin' and frothin' at the mouth? Did you get the paramedic guy over?'

'You didn't froth,' said Dougie. 'You just fell out of the tree and . . . yeah—went a bit spasmo. We thought you were coming over. Lizzie said you'd be OK, though. And she said you could see us as well, which was pretty cool.'

'I don't remember much about seeing anyone,' admitted Theo.

Dougie and Lizzie exchanged a look. 'Not even in the resuscitation room?' asked Dougie. 'You looked right at us!'

Theo scratched his head, baffled. 'What were *you* doing at the hospital?'

'Just helping out,' said Lizzie, getting off the

gravestone and stepping closer, eyeing him with fascination. 'That useless junior doctor decided you were dead when you weren't. I had to blow on her neck at about Gale-force nine to get her to notice that your heart was still beating.'

Theo began to feel as if he was in a dream. This conversation kept slipping around in a weird way, making him struggle to hang on to the thread of it. One minute these kids were making perfect sense and the next, they might as well have just slipped into another language.

'Why . . .' he gulped, '. . . would you have to *blow* on a junior doctor's neck?'

'Well, I would have *liked* to smack her round the head,' said Lizzie, putting her hands on her hips. 'She was being such an idiot! There are loads of stories about kids going into shutdown . . . the heartbeat slowing to one or two a minute. It's a primeval survival trick. She should have known all about that. If I *hadn't* breathed on her and given her some goosebumps she might never have looked back at the monitor and you'd be a goner.'

'Lizzie . . .' Theo took a deep breath. 'What *are* you on about?'

'She *couldn't* smack her round the head,' explained Dougie, his voice slow and patient. 'Because we can't *do* that kind of thing. The only thing we can do is move air around a bit and make you feel colder. If we try really hard.'

'It's one of the worst things about being a ghost,' said Lizzie. 'There are days when I want to slap someone so badly I just . . . evaporate!' She went a little transparent as she said this.

Theo's mind sent a message directly to his legs. For a moment his knees went weak and began to buckle. And in another moment he was running along the main path through the graveyard, his breath coming hard and fast and his heart bouncing around inside his chest. He was shouting something in between his ragged breaths. 'NO!' (puff) 'NO!' (puff) 'IT'S NOT . . .' (puff) 'REAL!'

Back on the path Dougie and Lizzie stood side by side, watching him.

'Well, that went well,' said Dougie.

CHAPTER EIGHT

Alisha sat under the tree in exactly the same place she'd been a week ago. She expected to feel a frisson of fear; an echo of the momentous thing which had happened to her.

But all she felt was . . . nothing. Just a bit of a warm breeze and the tickle of some blades of grass against her knee. She *did* feel a bit guilty for having left school. Would anyone have noticed she was missing yet? Would the school have rung home? Was Mum even now in a terrible panic, wondering where she'd gone?

No. She'd only been absent twenty minutes. It would take longer than that. She supposed she'd get into trouble . . . but maybe they would make allowances for her; say it was some kind of delayed reaction to her traumatic experience. That's probably what they'd say. Even though she was pretty much OK.

The tree above her seemed to be OK too—apart

from a seam of dark boiled sap down the side of its trunk and a streak of burnt leaves through the canopy. She and Theo would always be connected to this tree now, she guessed. She felt a pang again, thinking about Theo. Maybe she should find out where he lived, go round to his house and say sorry. She still wouldn't risk it at school—no matter how many volts had tried to fry her brain, she wasn't *insane*—but she owed him an apology. It would be really embarrassing, but she should do it. Maybe even today, if she could find out where he was.

And then she found out where he was.

He was tearing across the common towards her, like the hounds of hell were after him. Alisha sat bolt upright and stared nervously across the grass, shielding her eyes. Was he coming to have a go at her about what she'd said? Was he completely furious about it and just about to yell at her until her face melted?

But he wasn't even looking at her. He was just blindly running and looking . . . *absolutely terrified.* Alisha jumped to her feet and waved at him. 'THEO! What's up? What's the matter?'

Theo glanced around at her and then tripped over, fell face first into the grass and lay still.

'Sheesh!' Alisha ran across to him, skidding on to

her knees beside him. She poked him in the shoulder, wondering if he'd passed out—if there'd been a short circuit in his brain which had only just happened, days after the electrocution. But Theo rolled over on his side and stared at her, his face a mask of shock.

'What's going on?' she demanded. 'You look like you've seen a ghost!'

Theo sat up and knuckled his fists into his eyes. He seemed, in between the puffing and gasping, to be murmuring 'Not true, not true, not true!'

Alisha felt a wave of horror. 'Look . . . I'm sorry! I know it's not true! You're not a lame brain. It was just that Kirsty Fellows doing my head in and saying stupid things about you and me and—'

But Theo broke off from his muttering and stared at her as if she was mad. 'What?!'

'I shouldn't have called you a lame brain,' she said, looking him in the eyes. 'It wasn't nice and I didn't mean it.'

'Well . . . thanks,' he said. And he looked around him. He was very pale and shaky. Haunted. Suddenly he was staring fixedly over her right shoulder, his eyes round and shiny.

'But . . . that's not what this is about, is it?' Alisha cottoned on. 'Who was chasing you? Has someone been bullying you? Calling you names and stuff?'

'We certainly *didn't* call him names.' Alisha turned to see a boy and a girl standing a few metres away, looking concerned. 'We're not rude!' said the girl. 'We're just . . .'

'Ghosts,' said Theo with a gulp. 'You're ghosts.'

'We were trying to break it gently,' said Doug.

Alisha felt the skin across her arms and shoulders prickle, but she didn't know why. The boy and the girl looked perfectly normal—substantial. They weren't see-through or drifting above the ground or flickering.

'OK—is this some kind of joke?' she asked, glancing from Theo to the other two.

The other two—a boy and girl a couple of years older than them, wearing weird clothes—suddenly started grinning at each other.

'You can see us,' said the boy.

'I told you!' said the girl. 'I said they'd both see us! I knew it!' She clapped her hands in a jubilant way. 'She can see us perfectly!'

'Of *course* I can see you perfectly!' snapped Alisha, beginning to get quite exasperated. 'What is this? A Teenage Opticians outing? Is it some kind of eye test? Do you want to start backing away until I can't read the letters on your badges?' she demanded, peering at the collection on the girl's bib. 'B-A-Y-C-I-T-Y-R . . .'

'Oh and she's a funny one too!' squeaked the girl.
'That is just sooo groovy! We've got funny ones,
Dougie!'

Theo suddenly grabbed Alisha's arm. 'I'm going
to walk through them,' he said, in a wobbly voice.

Alisha shook him off exasperated. 'Theo! Is this a
joke because I called you a lame brain? I've already
said sorry!'

'Shut up,' said Theo. 'And just watch.'

The older boy and girl were looking more serious
now. 'Should we let him?' asked the boy. 'Will he be
OK?'

The girl shrugged as Theo made a beeline for him.
'Only one way to find out.'

The boy nodded and then stood still, stretching
out his arms as if he was planning to give Theo a
matey hug. 'Come on, then,' he said. 'Let's get it over
with. Try not to faint, eh?'

Theo glanced back at Alisha, his face still sweaty
and pale. Then he walked on.

And straight through the boy and out the other
side.

Where he fainted.

When Theo regained consciousness he could hear
voices. He glanced through a clump of wiry grass

and saw Alisha sitting on the ground with her head between her knees. 'I am not going to faint,' she was saying. 'I'm not going to faint.'

'No, that's good—just keep your head down— you'll be fine,' said Lizzie, kneeling next to her. 'I know it's a bit of a shock. Ha ha! Shock! Geddit? Aaah—maybe now's not the time.'

'She's going . . .' observed Doug, standing close by.

'I'm *not*!' insisted Alisha. 'I'm really not!'

'Good! Good for you!' said Lizzie. 'Girls are made of tougher stuff!'

Theo sat up and took a deep breath. If Alisha wasn't going to faint, he really needed to make sure *he* didn't in future. But when he remembered walking through Doug, goosebumps ran along his arms in waves. Stepping into the space which the boy *should* have occupied had felt like stepping into a deep freeze. He'd felt the chill rush through him and then his legs had buckled and everything had gone black.

'Oh, hello,' said Doug, noticing Theo had sat up. 'Sorry about that. I should probably have warned you. Living people do sometimes pass out when they wander through spirit people. Of course, most of them don't *know* that's why they've passed out. They just think it's flu or a funny turn. I thought if you could see me it might not be so bad . . .'

'How come you're not more see-through?' said Alisha, suddenly raising her head. Her cheeks were flushed and she looked quite cross. 'You're meant to be all see-through and wavery, not all coloured-in and normal-looking!'

'Well, to some people we *will* be a bit see-through,' said Lizzie, sitting down, cross-legged, beside her. 'Sensitive types sometimes get a glimpse of us but it's only ever a glimpse. You two are the first people to *really* see us in decades! It's amazing! We've never been able to talk to any living people before!'

Alisha took a long breath and then extended a trembling hand to touch Lizzie's beaming face. Her fingers went right through it and she gave a little squeak and then dropped her head back between her knees. 'I will not faint! I will not faint! I *will not* faint!'

And she didn't. Theo crawled through the grass (he didn't yet trust his legs to work properly) and sat beside her. Doug settled next to Lizzie and for a while all of them just stared at each other, saying nothing.

Eventually Theo said, 'OK . . . so how come we can see you when other people can't?'

'We think it was the lightning strike,' said Doug.

'It's changed you. Altered something in your brains. It's brilliant!'

'We can be in a club!' said Lizzie. 'We could call it Strike Club! Because we've all been struck by lightning.'

'You were struck too?' asked Alisha, her brown eyes wide. 'Really?'

'Yes! That's what killed us,' said Lizzie, cheerfully. 'Snap, crackle, and pop!'

Doug shrugged apologetically at them. 'She always makes the Rice Krispies joke.'

'So—you got struck too, only you didn't pop your clogs,' went on Lizzie. 'So we can be the Strike Club. I mean—you're a bit younger than us, but that's OK, we'll let you in. It's cool. Those kids in *The Double Deckers* are lots of different ages.'

Doug looked at her scornfully. '*The Double Deckers*? You *still* like *The Double Deckers*? It was pathetic at the time, but seriously—can't you move on?!'

Lizzie leapt to her feet and started boogying about singing 'Come aboard! Come aboard! Come aboard with the Double Deckers . . .'

Alisha was temporarily distracted from feeling TOTALLY FREAKED OUT by wondering what on earth Lizzie was singing. Theo, too, was peering at her in wonder.

'It's a very embarrassing TV series,' explained Doug, seeing their expressions. 'A bunch of kids with a den in a London bus. Didn't you ever see it?' They shook their heads. 'Ah well, a bit before your time, I guess. Count yourselves lucky.'

'. . . ticket . . . for a jouuuurney,' sang on Lizzie.

'Oh no!' Alisha suddenly looked horrified. 'Oh NO!'

Lizzie looked a bit crestfallen. 'I'm not *that* bad at singing.'

Alisha was on her feet. 'It's not you—it's *them*! It's Kirsty and Sophie. They're coming this way.' She glanced at Theo. 'We CANNOT let them see us!'

Theo followed Alisha's gaze and saw two girls from school heading up the main path of the common. They hadn't seen him and Alisha yet. He guessed they never would see Doug and Lizzie.

And then he realized Doug and Lizzie had vanished.

'The ghost kids are gone,' he murmured.

'So am I,' croaked Alisha, and ran away like a sprinter, leaving him dazed and confused beneath the tree.

CHAPTER NINE

Alisha ran all the way home. All the way, despite her sore feet. It took ten minutes and at no point did she stop and drop to a walk. By the time she'd hurtled indoors and up the stairs and landed on her bed, her heart was pumping at top speed. She lay on her back as her breathing gradually calmed down, and tried to work out how she was feeling.

Scared. She was feeling scared. She had never believed in ghosts and now—it seemed—she had to. Unless Theo and those kids were some kind of magic act . . . but no . . . she had only to remember Theo walking *right through* the boy called Doug to know that this could not be so.

She and Theo had met two ghosts. She felt like her brain was stretching, desperately trying to accommodate the intense *BIGNESS* of her discovery. So she was scared.

But also amazed. The world was no longer what it had been. And if this much had changed . . . how much *more* might change?

All this running was another change. She'd hardly noticed the effort. Her body and her feet were complaining enough right now but at the time it had seemed like the most natural thing in the world to do, as soon as she'd spotted Kirsty and Sophie.

She'd been on the verge of running, anyway. One more prickle of panic was all it took.

Alisha's emotions were confusingly mixed up. Scared about the ghosts. Fascinated about the ghosts. Amazed about the running. A bit ashamed of leaving Theo behind just because of Kirsty and Sophie. 'Seriously, though,' she said to herself, out loud. 'It's for the best. For him as much as me.' Her words sounded hollow, though. Why did she care so much about what other people thought? She should be tougher and just do as she wanted. She didn't even *like* Kirsty and her hangers-on that much. Why did it matter what they said?

And after what she'd just experienced, how could she even care any more?

She made up her mind that she would slip Theo a note the next day, arranging to meet again and talk properly about what they'd seen. As long as nobody saw her do it . . .

*

'Are you going with Alisha, then, Thunder Theo?' There was giggling and Theo looked around to see Kirsty and Sophie just behind him in the corridor as he gazed at the end-of-term summer disco poster. Aaah. *This* was what Alisha was getting so freaked out about.

He grinned at them and shrugged. 'Nothing's firmed up yet, ladies. I'm still available. Don't start fighting each other over me, though! It's upsetting.'

'In your dreams!' squeaked Kirsty and then she and Sophie went into fits of giggles and wandered off down the corridor. 'We wouldn't want to make Alisha *jealous . . .*' Kirsty called back, over her shoulder.

'You won't,' said Theo. And he was pretty sure about that. As soon as the ghost kids had vanished Alisha hadn't wanted to be seen anywhere near him. It didn't really hurt his feelings but he was annoyed with her. After what they'd just been through, you'd think she would want to talk about it! What they had seen on the common yesterday was way more important than stupid school stuff.

There was a gentle tug on his backpack and he turned in time to see Alisha walking away from him. 'Hey!' he called but she didn't look back. *Typical.* But then he noticed something in one of the little net pockets on the side of the bag: a folded up bit of paper. A note . . . ? He dug it out and opened it up.

Sorry about yesterday. Want to meet again on the common after school to talk? I'll go straight there and wait under the tree. A

Theo grinned. He had been planning to do exactly that himself. Immediately he felt better. He was *desperate* to talk about Doug and Lizzie. He had tried to talk to Mam about it last night but found that his words just kept drying up. What if she thought he was making it up—or worse, getting hallucinations? Dr Karish had warned them about glitches as their brains 'rebooted', and Alisha's parents had told his mam about her 'hallucinations' in the hospital.

He was so wrapped up in his thoughts as he wandered outside for lunch break that he nearly fell into a trench.

'*Oi! Look out!*' Theo jumped and noticed the yellow hazard tapes roping off the edge of the field. One of the builders, in a fluorescent vest and a hard hat, waved him away.

Theo paused. 'How far down are you digging?' he asked.

'All the way to Australia,' laughed the builder. 'At least it feels like it on a hot day like this!'

'Why do you need to dig down when you're meant to be building upwards?' asked Theo.

'Footings!' replied the builder, whose arms and shoulders were tanned and tattooed. 'All buildings need footings. And if it's a tall building you have to dig deeper footings to make sure it doesn't fall over.'

'Oh,' said Theo. 'Yeah—of course.' He peered into the trench and, despite the heat of the day, felt suddenly cold.

'Now—off you go,' said the man. 'If you fall in, I'll be getting in trouble!'

'OK, bye,' said Theo and headed back towards the playground where it was warmer.

'Have you been inspecting our building works?' came a friendly voice and Theo looked up to see Mr Carter smiling at him as he walked back across the playground, dodging a flying football.

'Yeah—sorry, sir—shouldn't have been there! The guy was just telling me,' said Theo.

'We've been waiting for this library extension for three years!' said Mr Carter. 'Our current library is little more than a corridor—a terrible state of affairs. Every school should have a good library at its heart, don't you think?'

'Um—yes,' agreed Theo, although he'd never been much of a reader. Too many words on a page just made his brain ache. 'They have to dig down a long way, don't they?' he added, glancing back at the builders as they toiled in the hot sun, flinging up spadefuls of earth.

'Yes—our footings have to go down a good four metres,' said Mr Carter. 'It's a two storey build and we need a little bit of basement storage too. It's all very disruptive in term time, but they'll be doing most of it across the summer holidays. Nearly here now! Just a few more days until the end of term— and what a start you've had, Theo. A school celebrity within days of your arrival!' He grinned broadly. 'I hope you'll be dancing all night at the end-of-term disco. You've got all that electrical energy to get out of your system!' He went away, chuckling at his joke.

Theo laughed with him. He liked his teacher. And the kids here were all OK too. They'd calmed down a bit about the whole-telly celebrity thing, but Conor and Ryan were still waving at him to join with their footy game at the other end of the playground. Alisha had apologized in her note and they would meet after school and talk about their amazing experience. He felt the sun warm him as he waved back at Conor and Ryan. Everything was OK.

So why, every time he glanced back at the building site, did he feel cold?

CHAPTER TEN

As soon as she was clear of the school gates Alisha had felt something inside her like the wind pushing a kite up into the air . . . and she had just *had* to run, holding her school backpack firm with its shoulder straps as she went.

All day she had been getting little spurts of nervous energy, fizzing away inside her. By home-time her insides felt like a bottle of lemonade which had been shaken violently and was ready to blow. But running released the pressure in a steady hiss and by the time she reached the tree she felt oddly calm.

'Hi,' said Theo, dropping down to sit beside her a couple of minutes later. 'I saw you running. I thought you said you were no good at it.'

'I *am* no good,' she said. 'I just . . . felt like it.'

'OK,' said Theo. 'So . . .'

'Yeah,' she tugged awkwardly at some daisies in the grass. 'Look . . . sorry about running off yesterday. It's just that I was freaked out . . .'

'Yeah, I get it. So was I,' he said. 'By the ghosts, though . . . not by Kirsty and Sophie!'

Alisha bit her lip. 'Look . . . Theo, I'm not like you. I can't stand all the attention and the teasing.'

'Whatever,' said Theo. 'But you should lighten up a bit. Make a joke of it. If you take it so seriously they'll only get worse.'

She knew he was right but it really wasn't that simple. 'Anyway,' she said. 'Doug and Lizzie. Did that *really* happen?'

'I could hardly sleep last night,' said Theo, excitement suddenly in his voice. 'I couldn't stop thinking about it. We met ghosts! We actually met real live ghosts!'

'Real *dead* ghosts,' corrected Alisha. She shivered—but it wasn't an unpleasant feeling. 'They weren't all that ghost*like* though, were they? They seemed quite normal. The girl—Lizzie—boogying about and singing . . .'

'Yeah, she was doing that the other day too, when I first met her.'

'You met her before?'

'Yeah, just here. The day before yesterday. She was climbing the tree. And disco dancing!' he added, with a snort. 'I offered to buy her an ice cream but she said no. I guess I know why now . . .'

'Hmmm, would've been a waste,' said Alisha and then giggled as she pictured Lizzie trying to lick an ice-cream cone and the whole thing just falling *through* her and splattering on the ground.

'But what about you?' Theo narrowed his eyes at her. 'What about your "hallucinations"? What did you see in the hospital?'

'Them,' said Alisha. 'Both of them. Nobody else could see them and the doctor said it was hallucinations.' She stared at him. 'Do you think it *is* hallucinations? I mean . . . our brains *were* fried, weren't they? Maybe that's all it is?'

'What . . . both of us seeing the same things? And having conversations with them?' protested Theo. 'How does *that* work? You can't just explain it away like that. It doesn't make sense, and anyway . . .' He pulled a bit of paper out of his bag. 'Read this . . .'

He handed Alisha a photocopy of an old newspaper cutting. It was dated 29 June, 1976. There were two separate photographs of teenagers—unmistakably Doug and Lizzie. The headline read:

GIRL AND BOY DIE BY LIGHTNING UNDER TREE

Alisha felt goosebumps wash across her skin as she read on.

Sheltering beneath a 60-foot oak tree on Easthampton Common, a schoolgirl and schoolboy were struck to death by lightning yesterday when a vicious storm hit the city on the hottest day of the year.

Elizabeth Margaret Holt (13) of Vale Dell Road and Douglas Crane (14) of Anglish Road, both died in a split second when the tree was struck.

Their bodies were found seconds later by two passing city council gardeners, who raised the alarm and did all they could to revive the children. One ran to the nearby Belleway Public House to telephone for an ambulance.

By the time the children arrived at the Royal Southern Hospital, however, each was pronounced dead.

'I saw their bikes resting on the grass nearby and then I saw them lying under the tree,' said Mr Albert Rowner, 22, of Oxford Street, Easthampton. 'They were lying with their feet towards the trunk as if they'd been blasted away from it. I sent my companion to the pub to call for an ambulance on the landlord's telephone, while I tried to revive them, but I was just too late. I don't think they can have suffered.'

The families of the children were notified by teatime and arrived at the hospital in time to hear the sad news.

Elizabeth Holt was planning to be a school teacher and Douglas Crane was hoping to join the RAF.

They had been swimming at the local lido before setting off for home on their bicycles.

Mr James Michaels, the headmaster of Hill Farm Comprehensive School, which the two friends attended, expressed the great shock of staff and pupils when they discovered what had happened.

'It's awful news,' said Mr Michaels. 'Most of their classmates were away for the day on a coach trip so they had no idea what had happened until yesterday evening or even this morning. Many of the girls are in tears. Doug and Lizzie were very well liked. We'll miss them terribly.'

'That's so sad,' breathed Alisha, feeling tears prickling at the back of her eyes. She handed the photocopy back to Theo. 'How did you find this?'

'I went down the *Echo* office after you ran off yesterday,' he said. 'Asked to look in their old cuttings files.'

'On your own? And they let you?' Alisha was impressed.

'Well, I just asked for that reporter who interviewed us last week and she was really helpful and introduced me to their library guy.'

'Oh no,' groaned Alisha. 'Not MORE newspaper

stuff. I'm only just getting over the last media frenzy!'

'I just said it was for school research,' said Theo. 'I got other stuff about them too.' He handed her several pages with assorted cuttings copied on to the white A4. Follow-up stories and an inquest report. 'Anyway, the main thing is we know they're not some kind of hallucination. They're real—and only *we* can see them. We've changed. Something in our brains has kind of rewired since the lightning strike.' He suddenly grinned and went into a mad croaky voice. 'WE SEE DEAD PEOPLE!'

'Oh stop it!' Alisha laughed and flapped the photocopies at him. Because it was scary . . . but he was funny too. 'Anyway . . . we might never see them again. It could be a temporary thing. I mean . . . they're not here now, are they?'

Theo gazed around in all directions. 'No. You could be right. They might have run out of ghost juice by now . . . they might not be able to make themselves seen again.'

'They might be standing right here now, shouting at us and we're not seeing or hearing them,' said Alisha. 'Lizzie might be blowing hard on the back of your neck . . . can you feel anything?'

Theo shrugged. 'Nope.' He looked crestfallen. 'What if that's *it* then?'

'Well . . . we can get back to normal, can't we?' said Alisha.

'Do you *want* to get back to normal?' he said.

She frowned, deep in thought. She couldn't be sure. The last couple of weeks had been so traumatic, but now she was sitting here in the warm sun, with everything she'd experienced, she wasn't sure she *did* want to go back to normal. Normal hadn't been so great.

'Come on,' said Theo. 'I'll show you the gravestone.'

He led her down to the far end of the common, where the sun-bleached grass gave way to a shady path through the old cemetery. It was peaceful and nobody was about apart from a middle-aged lady and her small terrier dog, walking along the path, staring at the ground. At the sound of their voices she glanced up and then peered at them both rather hard. Maybe she was expecting them to start kicking over headstones, thought Alisha. She smiled politely and the woman smiled back, obviously reassured.

'First time I've seen anyone else here!' said Theo, glancing over his shoulder at the woman as she and her dog ambled on. 'Well, anyone living. Anyway— this is one of the oldest graveyards in the city,' he went on, like a tour guide. 'It dates right back to the

1200s. I saw Doug and Lizzie here yesterday when I was looking at the headstone. I was totally freaked out when I realized they were ghosts. That's why I was running away. I thought I was going to chuck up, I was so scared!'

'I'm still scared,' said Alisha, as she traced her fingers across the gravestone inscribed with DOUGLAS CRANE and the dates and circumstances of his death. 'But I want to know more. I wish they'd show up again.'

Theo stood in the centre of the path, turning around slowly and calling: 'Doug! Lizzie! Are you here?'

They stood awhile in silence, listening to the chirruping of the birds, the gentle breeze in the trees, and a distant aeroplane as it crayoned a white line across the blue sky above them.

Nothing.

'You could be right,' said Alisha. 'I mean about the energy thing. I read a book about ghosts once which said they have to kind of feed off the energy of living people to make themselves visible . . . that's why people get chilled when they see them. They've just had all their body heat siphoned out of them.'

'I felt like I was in the Arctic when I walked through Doug yesterday,' admitted Theo.

'Were you scared?' asked Alisha.

'More shocked,' said Theo. 'I mean . . . I wanted to know the truth.'

Alisha was silent for a moment and then she said: 'You've changed too, haven't you? You were just some nutjob when I first met you, blabbering on about all that American president stuff and leaping about like a Jack Russell on a sugar rush. You're not like that now. Doing all this research!'

'Rewired,' said Theo, nodding. 'Both of us. Look at *you*, running! And you said you hated sports.'

They found they were grinning at each other.

'No,' said Alisha. 'I wouldn't go back to normal.'

'Me neither,' said Theo.

'Still, I don't think Doug and Lizzie are going to show up,' sighed Alisha. 'And there are so many things I want to ask them.'

'Well, let's just look about a bit—see if we can see them. They weren't up by the tree and they're not by Doug's grave . . . but they might hang out all over the common for all we know.'

They began to wander around the old cemetery, looking at the gravestones. Each one gave names and dates and sometimes words of comfort like 'Safe in the arms of Jesus' or 'At peace at last'. Some were new and easy to read while others were so ancient

Theo had to trace the lettering with his fingers and try to work out what it said by touch.

Alisha crouched down by a low, black marble grave, half hidden by ivy. Above her stretched a tall hedge of yew trees with dark-green needle-shaped leaves. There was a row of very old headstones beneath the hedge. They seemed to have sunk into the earth, but Alisha guessed the earth had probably just built up around them over the years, slowly burying the stones and their chiselled messages of sadness, loss, hope, and comfort, from the bottom up.

Then, with a start, she saw that someone was crouched over a grave at the end of the row. It was hard to tell in the dim light beneath the yews, but it looked like an old woman in a grey dress. And Alisha realized, with a thud of her heart, that the old woman was crying. Well, of *course,* she was. This was a graveyard! People came here to mourn their dead.

Alisha snapped a twig underfoot and the woman jumped and began to turn around.

'Sorry,' said Alisha. 'I didn't mean to disturb you.'

The woman's face was pale. Her skin was papery thin and her hair was long and white. She gathered a shawl around her thin shoulders and peered at Alisha in astonishment.

Theo put a hand on Alisha's shoulder at exactly the

point that she realized. 'She's . . . she's see-through,' he whispered. Chills rushed through Alisha and she found she could not look away from the apparition in front of her. She had not bargained for this. She had just got her head around the idea of Doug and Lizzie—who looked so real and talked to them like normal kids—being ghosts. That had scared her enough but now, just four or five metres away, stood a *proper* ghost. A classic 'grey lady'. And it was staring RIGHT into Alisha's eyes.

'I—I'm sorry,' she gasped, again.

'Who are you?' said Theo, over her shoulder. 'Can you talk to us?'

The woman's solemn eyes—of no colour that Theo could work out—shifted across to him. She still looked astonished and not entirely friendly. 'We mean you no harm,' gulped Theo. 'We know other ghosts around here . . . Doug and Lizzie . . . have you met them? They're a bit more . . . dense . . . than you.'

The woman drew her shawl in tighter still and then raised a long, skinny finger and pointed at her throat. A second later she evaporated into a drift of grey mist.

Alisha found she was making weird sucking, gasping noises and realized that for the past minute or so she had forgotten to breathe.

'Who are you calling dense?' came a voice behind them and they spun around to see Lizzie sitting high up on a small mausoleum, swinging her white-socked legs.

Alisha was amazed to find relief *flooding* through her. Lizzie looked so familiar and so real. 'You're back!' she exclaimed. 'We thought you might not come back again!'

'Is that why you were bothering poor Ivy?' said Lizzie, tying her beads into a knot.

'You saw her too?' asked Theo. 'Who is she?'

'Ivy Goodwin—died in 1878,' said Alisha. 'Bit of a moper.'

'She saw *us*,' said Theo. 'She looked right at us. Scared me to death!' He let out a long breath and Alisha was pleased he'd admitted it. She'd been scared to death too.

'Well, I'm sure she did see you—she just wasn't expecting you to see *her*,' said Lizzie. 'Bit of a shock for the old dear.'

'Why did she do that pointing thing?' asked Theo. 'She pointed at her throat.'

'Oh, she died of diphtheria,' said Lizzie, breezily. 'It gets you in the throat. Loads of people got it back then. Quite a few of them show up on visits here. It's a kind of Diphtheria Death Club. Like our Strike Club but with more coughing. Strike Club is much groovier. And much harder to get into. I mean, if you haven't had 70,000 volts go through you, you can't join. Anyone can catch a disease but only a chosen few get fried by lightning.'

'Only *you* could think getting struck by lightning is *groovy*.'

Alisha and Theo spun around to find Doug just behind them.

'Hi,' he said, with a little wave. 'Sorry—did I make you jump?'

'You're a ghost,' said Theo. 'It's your job.'

Doug laughed. 'That's more like it! Have you stopped all the running away and shouting and fainting now?'

Theo looked at Alisha. She was still getting over Ivy Goodwin, but she seemed quite OK with Doug and Lizzie now. He found he was beaming around at them all. 'Yeah!' he said. 'We're OK.'

'They can see the other ghosts!' Lizzie told Doug. 'But we found them first. The others will all be so jealous we've got hauntees who talk back! This is *so groovy*!'

'Liz, please STOP saying groovy all the time,' said Doug. 'Nobody says that any more. You sound like you're stuck in a *Scooby-Doo* cartoon!'

'Jeepers!' squeaked Lizzie in a bad American accent.

'Hauntees?' echoed Alisha. 'You call us *hauntees*?'

'Well, that's what you are. We *are* haunting you,' said Lizzie with a matter-of-fact shrug. 'You're not just any hauntees, of course. You're special. We can talk to you.'

Theo stepped closer to her, tilted his head to one side, and waved his hand through her face.

'Do you *mind*?' She waved her hand back through *his* face. 'Honestly! You twenty-first-century boys have no manners!'

'Wait,' said Alisha, taking a deep breath. 'I haven't done this yet. Sorry, Doug—I just need to know.' And she carefully put her hand right through his chest. At once a cold, tingly chill ran up her arm and scattered more goosebumps across her shoulder. Doug grinned at her and waved his ghostly hand through her head. Spangles of coolness shuddered through her cheeks and scalp.

'OK? Not going to faint?' checked Doug. He was quite thoughtful for a dead boy, Alisha thought. She found she was beaming at him.

Theo suddenly did a whoop and then a cartwheel down the mossy path. He leapt back on to his feet, laughing.

'Me and Alisha have decided,' he puffed. 'This Strike Club thing . . . ? We're in!'

CHAPTER ELEVEN

'Kirsty says do you want to come over and sit with us?'

Alisha glanced up from her plate, surprised to see Sophie standing over her, smiling. At the next table along, Kirsty and a couple of other girls were waving at her and looking friendly. Alisha didn't trust this . . . but a little part of her lit up inside. She so wanted to be included. Another part of her wanted to ask Sophie why Kirsty had to send a messenger as if she was a queen dispatching one of her courtiers. But she didn't need to ask. Kirsty *was* a queen and Sophie was a lady-in-waiting. Any idiot could work that out.

Still . . . it might be nice to visit the palace. There had been no more teasing about Theo for a while so maybe they'd got over that. Alisha smiled back, gathered up her bag and her tray and left the table where she'd been eating alone.

If she was honest she would have to admit to herself that she'd rather be sitting with Theo, talking about their time on the common as members of the newly created Strike Club. But Theo knew how embarrassed she got and although he'd come into the dining hall, he'd only given her a brief smile and then sat down with Conor Bales and Ryan Tasker. Theo was good at fitting in.

'So—how are you?' asked Kirsty, as soon as Alisha had taken the seat opposite her.

'OK,' said Alisha. 'My feet are nearly back to normal now—apart from the pattern. That might stay for good, the doctor says.'

'The pattern?' asked Kirsty. 'What pattern?'

'It's called a Lichtenberg figure,' said Alisha. 'It's the pattern the lightning left as it blasted through our feet. There's a bit on my shoulder too, where the strike went in.' She pulled up the left sleeve of her polo shirt and showed them the pale-red tree-like tattoo at the top of her arm.

'Wow,' said Sophie, looking genuinely intrigued. 'That's so cool . . . like Harry Potter's scar.'

'Yes,' said Alisha. 'But as far as I know, it hasn't given me any magical powers against dark wizards.'

The girls giggled. 'You're so funny, Alisha,' said Kirsty. 'So . . . are you looking forward to the school disco? You are going, aren't you?'

Uh-oh, here we go, thought Alisha. *They'll start*

with the Theo stuff again now. 'Yes, I'll be going,' she said, adding quickly: 'What are you all wearing?'

'Well,' said Kirsty. 'Because it falls on Friday the thirteenth, we thought we'd go spooky style. I'm going as a vampiress.'

'I'll be a witch—but a beautiful one,' declared Sophie. 'I've got this gorgeous black satin dress.'

The others put their bids in for an assortment of undead glamour and Alisha found herself actually enjoying the conversation. She knew it was temporary. The cool girls would get tired of her soon, but she might as well enjoy it for now. 'I've got a white dress,' she said. 'I could go as a ghostly girl.' She grinned at them, especially Emma and Rosie who had SO wanted to mourn her passing on TV. 'After all, I nearly got to be one.'

'Oooh yes—I can help with your ghostly make-up!' said Kirsty. 'Everyone can come round my place beforehand and get ready.' There were squeaks of enthusiasm from the other girls and Alisha felt a fizz of pleasure to be included. Kirsty was OK, really. As long as she didn't start up about Theo again.

After lunch they had sports and played rounders out on the playground. For the first time *ever*, Alisha scored a rounder. She actually hit the ball with the bat—a satisfying crack resounding through the warm afternoon air—and then ran *all the way round.* Instead of the usual wails of frustration, the other kids were cheering her on. Alisha almost felt like she belonged. She was laughing with delight as she skidded into fourth base to cheers and applause.

'. . . assassin of the Archduke was a student by the name of . . . THEO, I'm sorry. Am I boring you? Is there something more gripping out of the window?'

Theo jumped and stared guiltily at Mr Carter, who was eyeing him with frustration. He liked Mr Carter's lessons but he'd just seen Alisha score a rounder. *Alisha!* Who was terrible at sports!

'Sorry, sir,' he mumbled. 'I was only looking out for a few seconds.'

'So . . . you'll know everything we were just talking about?' said Mr Carter, raising one eyebrow at Theo.

'Um—yeah—I think so.'

'OK then—so who assassinated Archduke Franz Ferdinand in 1914?'

'A student,' began Theo.

'. . . by the name of?'

'Oh—er—Gavrillo Princip, sir. Of the Black Hand Gang. It was his second go at it. He was meant to shoot the Archduke earlier that day but he bottled out of it and then went up the pub for a drink . . . and then the Archduke and Archduchess's chauffeur drove them the wrong way home and the car went past the pub and Gavrillo Princip saw it and had another go and POP—dead Archduke and Archduchess and BANG—World War One!'

There was a stunned silence and then a broad smile broke over Mr Carter's face. 'Well, Theo—if staring out of the window does *that* for your memory for history, I shan't complain.'

The lesson moved on and Theo sat in a strange cloud of astonishment. How had *that* happened? Well . . . he'd heard it all earlier in the lesson, of course, but to be able to remember it with all that detail? Normally stuff like that went into one ear, did a cartwheel across his brain, blew a raspberry and went out the other. It was true. He and Alisha *were* changed.

Mr Carter caught up with him in the corridor at the end of the day.

'Theo—I think you may have a bit of a gift for history,' he said. 'Have you been watching the History Channel at home or something?'

Theo shrugged. 'No—although I do like the stories. I mean . . . that's what history is, isn't it? Stories . . . but with real people. Dead and gone people. Sometimes,' he found himself talking as much to himself as to his teacher, 'it seems like the dead are still with us.'

'Immortalized in books, paintings and documentaries,' said Mr Carter. 'Well—keep it up, Theo. You've been quite a surprise!' He headed off down the corridor. Theo wished he could run after the teacher and tell him what had happened on the common, but that was never going to be possible. He and Alisha had agreed that they would not tell anyone about their new friends.

'They just won't believe it,' Alisha had said as they'd walked home yesterday. 'Remember when I saw Doug and Lizzie at the hospital? They thought my brain was fried. Nobody else can see them so nobody else will ever believe us.'

'OK,' Theo had said. 'So—the first thing you need to know about Strike Club is that you don't talk about Strike Club.'

'Agreed.' Alisha had held up her hand for an awkward high five and he'd slapped his palm against it before they went their separate ways.

Theo was looking forward to another Strike Club meeting. Yesterday's get-together in the graveyard hadn't lasted much longer after he'd made his announcement about joining Strike Club. Lizzie and

Doug had got a bit see-through and said their energy was getting low. It was frustrating because he and Alisha had so much to ask them about what it was like to be a ghost—but they'd all agreed to meet up by the tree again today.

'Eat a good lunch!' Lizzie had called to them, as she faded out against the wrought iron cemetery gates. 'We can nick some of your energy if you've got plenty of it to spare.'

Theo *had* eaten a good lunch and he'd noticed Alisha tucking in too, sitting with those girls that she'd run away from the other day. It seemed like they were all good friends again now. *Girls.* He'd never understand them.

At the doorway to the playground a stream of kids flowed out, heading home, carrying bags and blazers. Pushing back through the flow was one of the builders, carrying a small chunk of stone. He made his way up the corridor towards Mr Carter, who was about to enter the staffroom.

'Here—sir!' called the builder, whom Theo recognized as the man he'd chatted to by the footings. 'Can you read Latin?'

Mr Carter paused, looking surprised. It wasn't the kind of question you expected from a builder, thought Theo, watching them. 'Well . . . a bit,' said

Mr Carter. 'I'm not the world's best but I did study it at A level many years ago. What have you got?'

'Just dug this up,' said the builder. He handed the chunk of stone—about the size of a paperback book—to the teacher and Mr Carter peered at it curiously. Theo could see there was some angular lettering chiselled into the grey rock, which was old and dirty. Mr Carter glanced up and saw his pupil staring. 'Theo,' he said. 'Take a look. This must be pretty old.'

Theo stepped across and peered at the stone. He couldn't make any sense of the lettering, which was faded and chipped away in places. 'What does it say, sir?' he asked, fascinated. The letters he could make out read:

unqua . . . cio . . . pro . . . ligeo . . .

. . . but it was obvious they were incomplete.

'Yeah,' said the builder. 'Can you read it?'

Mr Carter laughed at their eager faces. 'Well,' he said. 'It's been a while since I've had two such keen history students paying me this much heed! Well, I'm not sure—er—'

'Chris,' said the builder.

'—Chris . . . I'm not sure because it's broken at an angle and this bit is only half a word, but it does *look* like "Never . . . *something* . . . God . . . (God-fearing?) . . . lest . . . or unless . . ." and . . . well, that's where my knowledge runs out, really. Sorry. Did you find any more?'

'Nope—that's all. I'll keep an eye out, though,' said Chris, rubbing his sun-freckled nose and looking a bit disappointed. 'What do you think it is?'

'Oh—probably a bit of an old church building or masonic hall or somesuch,' said Mr Carter. 'I'd like to think it was something much more exciting, but the city council archaeological department told us there was nothing much of interest in this area . . . that's why we've been able to get you all working so fast. In some areas you can't build a shed without a full archaeological dig for months beforehand. Still . . . you never know what might turn up. Do let me know if you find anything else. Can I keep this for the school's history display or would you like to hang on to it, Chris?'

'Nah—you keep it for the kids to see,' said Chris, 'I'd better get back to work. I'll let you know, though, if I dig up anything else.'

'Thank you!' called Mr Carter as Chris marched back along the corridor. 'Well, Theo—can you take this back to class and leave it on my desk? I would go myself but there's a cup of tea in this staffroom with my name on it—and if I don't drink it in the next thirty seconds my brains will dribble out of my nose. That's what teaching Year 6 does for you.'

Theo laughed and held out both hands and the teacher dropped the stone into them and turned away. 'Thanks, Theo. See you tomorrow,' he said and the staffroom door closed behind him. If he'd glanced back he would have noticed that Theo had suddenly turned a shade paler and his hands were trembling.

Theo hurried back to the classroom. He was desperate to put the stone down on Mr Carter's desk and get away from it. As soon as it had made contact with his skin he had felt a dark chill. It was like the chill he'd felt when he'd stared into the footings— but much, much worse. It was very different to the tingling coolness he felt around Doug and Lizzie. He did not like it. Not at all.

CHAPTER TWELVE

'I wouldn't have come,' said the woman. 'I-I didn't plan to. But then, once I realized where you lived, I found myself just walking here. I didn't seem to be able to stop.' She laughed a little shakily and the teacup rattled in the saucer. Mam's best china.

Theo still had no idea who this was or why she was here. The second he had raced through the door, back from school, Mam had called him into the front room and introduced him to a complete stranger called Mrs Rathbone. She was a plump, fair-haired woman—in her fifties he would guess—in a grey skirt and purple top. Behind small spectacles her eyes were a little red-rimmed and there was something vaguely familiar about her. Her dog, Barney, sat quietly at her feet. Suddenly Theo realized it was the woman with the terrier that he and Alisha had seen at the cemetery yesterday. Yet . . . he'd barely glanced at her. There was something else . . .

'I saw you on the news of course, Theo,' said Mrs

Rathbone. 'It was quite a shock. Sorry, that's not a play on words!' she added. 'I mean . . . it was a shock for me. But even so, I wasn't thinking about coming to see you. I probably wouldn't have, but then, this morning, the *Echo* called me.'

Theo was still confused. He wanted to ask what was going on but Mam was giving him The Look That You Dare Not Defy. *Shut up and wait,* was what the look was saying today.

'They called me because of the research you were doing,' said Mrs Rathbone, taking a small sip of tea. 'About what happened in 1976. They thought I might like to talk about it. I said no thanks.'

Theo couldn't hold on any longer. 'Why—why would they call you? Did you know Lizzie and Dougie?'

Now it was Mam's turn to try butting in. 'What? Who?' she said but Mrs Rathbone was nodding already. 'I did know Lizzie,' she said. 'And I knew Dougie. He . . . he was my big brother.'

Now Theo could see the likeness; the familiarity. When she smiled her mouth went a bit lopsided . . . just like Dougie's. And her greeny-brown eyes were just the same, too, even though she looked thirty or more years older than her ghostly brother.

Theo felt swamped. His skin was prickling with

goosebumps and his throat was thick with sadness. Until now it had been easy to think of Doug as just a slightly see-through mate with an interesting past. But this made it all different. Mrs Rathbone . . . decades ago . . . had lost her big brother. When she was just a kid.

'I'm really sorry,' said Theo. 'About what happened to him.'

Mam suddenly shook her head. 'Oh—I see! This is the boy who died in the seventies, you were telling me about, Theo. Oh, Mrs Rathbone, I'm so sorry.'

'No, really, please don't be,' said the woman. 'And please call me Karen, if I'm calling you Jenna! I should apologize to you really, just showing up like this after everything you've been through. It's just that . . .' She gulped. 'When he died, and ever since, I've never stopped thinking about . . . what happened to him. I mean . . . did he suffer or did he . . . ?' She gulped again, putting down her tea, and Mam handed her a tissue from the box on the coffee table.

'You wanted to ask me what it was like?' said Theo. 'To be struck by lightning.'

'I'm sorry,' she said, blowing her nose. 'I have no right to ask you anything; you must be quite traumatized enough.'

'No—no, really, it's fine,' said Theo. 'I can tell you. I don't mind.'

She smiled at him, lopsided like Dougie.

'I didn't really feel any pain,' said Theo. 'Just a big kind of shove, like something whacking into me. And I could see a pink-white light and smell burning. When I came to in the hospital I was sore and achey— but that's all. I don't think Dougie would have felt a thing. He wouldn't have had time to.'

He longed to add: 'And actually he's fine—and really cool—and hanging out with me and Alisha and Lizzie. I'm seeing him in about half an hour.' But of course, he didn't.

'It's funny . . .' said Karen Rathbone. '. . . the way you call him Dougie. And you call Elizabeth Lizzie. That's what everyone called them—but it wasn't in the newspapers. They were always Douglas and Elizabeth in print.'

'Um . . . well, I suppose I feel like I know them . . . in a way,' burbled Theo. 'Reading about them . . .'

'I wish you could have known Dougie,' she said. 'He was the tops. Even though we were always fighting and . . .' She paused, screwing her eyes up and drawing in a deep breath. '. . . it's such a shame we were fighting on his last day.'

'Oh Karen,' Mam said, reaching over to touch her

arm. 'You've been carrying this nearly all your life; that's so sad. It must have been horrible to lose your brother so suddenly. How old were you?'

'I was ten,' sniffed Karen. 'And yes . . . losing him was awful. Watching what it did to my parents was probably worse; they never really got over it. But, bless them, they're both gone now and probably they've met up with Dougie in the next world. It's only me left now . . . and . . . I just wish I'd had a better last day with him.'

Theo and his mother exchanged glances. 'What happened?' asked Mam, softly.

'We had a row, right before he went off to school,' said Karen. 'I said something horrible to him. And it turned out to be the last thing.'

'But you *must* forgive yourself for that,' said Mam. 'Kids say stupid, horrible things to each other all the time—especially brothers and sisters. I bet, wherever Douglas is, the last thing he would want is for you to feel so bad.'

'That's what I tell myself,' said Karen. 'And on my good days, I believe it.' She took a deep breath and stood up. 'But thank you—thank you both so much. Theo,' she held out her hand and he took it. 'What you have told me has really, really helped. People have always said, *oh, he would have known nothing about it* but I could never be certain. Now I've spoken to you . . . I can believe it.'

'I'm really glad we could help,' said Mam. 'And look—we're only a few streets away. Any time you need to talk, please drop by. We're connected now, aren't we?'

'That's very kind of you,' said Karen, gathering her handbag and getting Barney to his feet.

'I mean it. I always work from home in the afternoons so I'm usually here. It's just me and Theo,' she added, ruffling her son's wild hair.

'I may well do that,' smiled Karen. 'Thank you both so much.'

They saw the woman and her dog out and then Mam hugged him. 'That was lovely, Theo,' she said. 'You were so kind to her. I'm really proud of you. Now . . . what are you going to do? A bit of gaming? I don't mind—you can have an hour—even though it's school tomorrow. You deserve it.'

Theo grinned and shook his head. 'I'm going up the common to see some mates,' he said.

'Are you sure you're up to it?' asked Mam.

'Yes!'

He left the house minutes later, feeling very, very strange about the past half hour. It had never occurred to him that Doug might have a living relative right here in the neighbourhood. He wondered whether to say anything. Maybe Lizzie's family were around too. Maybe he and Alisha should be passing messages along to them, like those TV psychics. He pictured himself on a stage in a suit, tapping his temples, eyes closed, murmuring 'Is there someone here called Bill? Ben? Billy-Bob . . . ? I'm getting the letter "B" . . . or it might be "C".'

Maybe not.

CHAPTER THIRTEEN

'So . . . why are you still here?'

Alisha and Lizzie lay on the grass near the banks of the ornamental lake. Closer to the water, Doug was trying to explain to Theo why fishing was such a great hobby. For Theo—a boy who could barely sit still for five minutes—it wasn't easy to grasp.

'Sorry—that sounded rude,' added Alisha, because Lizzie wasn't answering. She was just lying there, playing with her knotted string of beads and smiling into the sky. 'I mean . . . why hang around here when there's the whole of heaven to visit . . . or the universe to float through . . . ? Not that I *want* you to go, of course.'

'We like it here,' said Lizzie, simply. 'We used to come here all the time on our bikes, me and Doug, when we were living.'

'Is Doug, like, your boyfriend?' asked Alisha, quietly.

Lizzie snorted. 'Doug?! You're kidding me! No way. My heart belongs to Donny.'

'Donny? Who's that?'

Lizzie stared at her like she was simple. '*Donny! Osmond!*'

'Ooooh,' said Alisha. '*That* Donny. Yeah—I heard about the Osmonds. A seventies boy band.' She grinned. 'Nothing changes.'

'"The Twelfth of Never" is my favourite Donny song,' said Lizzie. 'Soooo dreamy.' She started humming a slow ballad and rocking gently to and fro.

'He's still going, you know,' said Alisha. 'He's in musicals in the West End sometimes. My nan saw him in something. Have you seen him lately? I mean . . . in pictures or anything?'

Lizzie shook her head with a sad smile. 'It's too painful,' she admitted. 'Seems like only last week he was a teenage heart-throb . . . and now he's a flippin' granddad. I prefer to remember him as he was . . .'

Alisha did some mental arithmetic. 'So . . . you're thirteen, right? And you died in 1976 . . . so . . . if you'd lived you'd now be . . .'

'Yeah, all right!' snapped Lizzie. 'Old enough to be *your* granny! And old grandpa Donny would still look hot to me. I know. You don't have to rub it in.'

Alisha laughed but then The Question came back.

She *had* to ask The Question. It had been in her head for the last couple of days. 'So . . . Lizzie . . . is there a God?' she murmured. She clenched her fists and breathed out slowly, waiting for the life-changing answer.

Lizzie shrugged. 'I suppose so . . .'

Alisha sat up and peered at Lizzie closely. She could feel the coolness which she knew was Lizzie very gently tapping into her own energy field. She didn't mind. In fact she was beginning to quite like it on this hot day. 'Lizzie! Tell me! Is there a GOD?!'

'There is . . . something,' said Lizzie. 'But it's not as straightforward as that. And I haven't met it yet so I don't really know.'

'Oh come *on*!' Alisha waved her hands in frustration. 'The biggest deal in the *world* and you don't even bother to find out?!'

'Thing is,' said Lizzie. 'Once I'm ready to find out, I will. But it'd mean leaving this place. Maybe even leaving Doug, if he doesn't come along with me. Once spirits decide to move on and find out . . . well, they don't ever come back. As far as I know. One day I'll go. Just not yet. I'm happy here.'

'But what do you do all day? Do you sleep at night? Do you go and visit your relatives?'

Lizzie shook her head. 'Not any more. I did a few

times but it was too depressing. Either they were all sitting around moping, which was depressing, or they were trying really hard to have a good time . . . without me . . . which was depressing. Anyway, I haven't got any brothers or sisters—and Mum and Dad passed over years ago. I'll catch up with them one day. They're OK.'

'How do you know?' asked Alisha. 'Did you speak to them?'

'No—they went straight on,' said Alisha. 'But they know I'm OK. I just know they do . . . can't really explain how. They know I'll catch up.'

'What about Dougie?' asked Alisha.

'Word of advice,' said Lizzie, narrowing her eyes. 'Don't ask.'

'O . . . K,' said Alisha, feeling she'd maybe pried too much. 'So . . . how do you pass the time? Don't you get bored?'

'No! It's been brilliant,' said Lizzie. 'Sometimes it feels like only weeks since we came over. There's loads to do . . . people to watch, wildlife to study, iPads to mess with.'

'iPads?' spluttered Alisha. 'You know about iPads?!'

'Yeah—of course!' grinned Lizzie. 'Brilliant invention! People sit around on the common, surfing the internet, gaming, watching movies and listening to music. We just hang over their shoulders and join in. Of course, we do mess up the screen a bit sometimes, which is annoying. Electromagnetic field and all that . . . but usually it's OK if we're upwind. We drain the batteries a bit, so we don't start watching a movie unless the iPad's fully charged.'

Alisha stared at her in amazement. 'But you . . . you're such a seventies girl! How have you got your head around all this new stuff?'

'I may be stuck in seventies clothes,' said Lizzie, looking slightly affronted, 'but I'm not stuck in the *decade*!'

'That's what she tells *you*,' said Doug, ambling over with Theo. 'She's still nuts about Donny Osmond.'

'I'm *over* him!' said Lizzie, quickly darting her eyes at Alisha.

'Your secret's safe with me,' whispered Alisha, with a giggle.

'Oh yeah—you've moved on to Les out of the Bay City Rollers,' sniggered Doug.

'I was NEVER into Les from the Bay City Rollers!' yelled Lizzie, looking horrified.

Doug shook his head sadly at Alisha and Theo. 'She has appalling taste in music. She doesn't get Bowie at *all*.'

'Bowie . . . ?' asked Theo. 'Oh—you mean *Ground-control-to-Major-Tom* guy . . . ?

'Yes! I *knew* you'd know,' said Doug. '"Space Oddity". Best song of 1975.'

'Space . . .' Theo looked thoughtful. 'Doug—can *you* . . . you know . . . go up into space?'

There was a pause as Doug considered his words with a frown. 'Why would I want to do that . . . ?'

'To see what's out there!' said Theo.

'Well, nothing is out there. The clue is in the name,' said Doug. 'Space!'

'It's the God thing,' said Lizzie, sounding a little tired. 'He really wants to ask about the God thing.'

'Oh,' said Doug. 'Well . . . sorry . . . but we don't know yet. We haven't looked.'

'Why not?' demanded Theo.

'Well,' said Doug, 'If there *is* a God, I might have to ask him why he sent a lightning bolt to kill us. It wouldn't be a good start would it?' He fell silent and gazed away into the middle distance. Lizzie did the same. Theo turned to follow their gaze. They were looking at a tree.

Just a short walk from the lake, long since grown over with ivy and crowded with young holly saplings, the stunted dead oak raised a solitary broken branch to the sky.

'Was that where you got struck?' Theo asked, as Alisha also turned to look.

'Yep—right there,' said Doug. 'It was one of the hottest summers on record. Went right up to ninety-six degrees! And it hadn't rained for weeks and weeks. Cows were dropping dead in fields and roads were melting.'

'We'd just been down the lido after school,' said Lizzie. She smiled, apparently lost in a memory. 'We loved the lido!'

'What's a lido?' asked Theo.

'It's an outdoor pool—sometimes fed by the sea,' explained Alisha. 'Easthampton had one back in the seventies. They closed it down in the eighties, Mum says. So—Lizzie—Doug—go on!'

'We'd cycled back and then it started raining cats and dogs,' went on Doug. 'So we dumped our bikes on the ground and stood under the tree. Then . . . bang . . . game over.'

'Did it hurt . . . dying?' asked Alisha, in a low voice.

'Didn't feel a thing,' said Doug. 'The only reason you two felt a thing was because you *didn't* die.'

'Good,' said Theo, with feeling. 'That's good. So . . . how did you even know you *were* dead? Did you start floating about?'

'I can't really remember,' said Doug. 'It's all a bit foggy.'

'Me neither,' said Lizzie, with a shrug. 'It takes a while to sort of get yourself tuned in. By the time we'd done that all the fuss was over.'

'So . . . you didn't go to your own funeral,' said Alisha.

'No,' said Doug. He smiled tightly and looked away. 'Can we change the subject?'

'OK,' said Theo. 'Answer this one: can you go anywhere you like? Around the world?' He pictured Doug and Lizzie zooming around the planet like Superman and visiting exotic locations.

'We can only go to places we went to when we were alive,' said Doug. 'And the further we go from the place where we were last alive, the weaker our energy gets. That's why we stay here mostly.'

Alisha looked around. It was a nice place to stay. She thought she might want to do the same . . . for a while. 'I should go home, now,' she said, with a reluctant sigh. 'Mum will get worried. I'm quite tired too.'

'Yeah—I'm wrecked!' said Theo, running his fingers through his spiky hair. 'I suppose we're still recovering.'

Doug and Lizzie exchanged guilty glances.

'Um . . . that's probably our fault,' admitted Doug. 'We should have gone about ten minutes ago . . . when our energy ran out . . .'

'But we were having so much fun talking to you,' said Lizzie, biting her lip. 'So we've been kind of . . . borrowing from you.'

'You mean you're sucking up all our energy?' said Theo, rolling his eyes. 'Well I like *that*! You didn't even ASK!'

'Sorry,' said Lizzie, fading out. 'We won't do it again.'

Doug faded with her, his face rueful. 'See you tomorrow, maybe?' he called and his voice was much quieter.

'Yes!' yelled back Theo and Alisha together.

When their friends had gone they stared at each other. 'This is . . . so amazing,' said Theo.

Alisha nodded. 'Tomorrow . . . we must eat more lunch.'

CHAPTER FOURTEEN

Theo woke with a start. It was dark. And cold.

Which, on a July night, under a duvet, it shouldn't be.

He checked the clock on his bedside table—2.38 a.m. Then he glanced around and found Doug, sitting on his bed, sending out a cool draught like an open freezer.

'Doug! What are you doing here?' he asked.

'I wanted to say thanks,' said the apparition—and he did *look* apparition-y, this far from the common. Pale blue and glowing. 'You were nice to KJ.'

Theo rubbed his face and sat up in bed. Although he pulled the duvet across, Doug did not slide with it, but remained sitting still while the material travelled through him.

'Who's KJ?' he asked, keeping his voice low in case Mam, in the next room, heard him.

'My little sister,' said Doug.

'Oh—*Karen*!' said Theo. 'Mrs Rathbone.'

Doug winced. 'She's always been KJ to me—short for Karen Jeanette.'

'So . . . you check in on her, then?' asked Theo.

Doug nodded. 'From time to time; see how she's doing. She was talking to Barney about you when I checked in a few hours ago.'

'Does she know you're there?' asked Theo.

Doug shrugged. 'She can't see me.'

'How is she doing?' asked Theo. He didn't want to talk about the sadness he'd seen in Karen's eyes.

'OK, I guess,' said Doug. He didn't sound convinced. 'You saw her. What did you think?'

Theo sighed. 'I don't know—'appen all the stuff about me and Alisha has brought up some old feelings. It must be hard losing your brother.'

'I made it worse,' said Doug.

'How do you mean?' asked Theo. 'How could you make it worse? You're dead!'

'No . . . before. The last day. I was really mean to her.'

'She said she was mean to *you*,' said Theo.

But Doug shook his head. 'She was just a kid. I nicked her favourite Sindy doll—the ballerina one—and dropped it in the garden pond. She was really, really angry. Why wouldn't she be? She loved that doll and I'd just turned it into the Creature from the Black Lagoon.'

'So . . . what happened?'

'She shouted at me and I just laughed at her—she was so pink in the face. Then I grabbed my bike to go to school.'

'And . . . ?' prompted Theo. 'What did she do?'

'Nothing. It was what she said.' In the dim light that shone in from the street lamp outside, Theo thought he saw a tear track down Doug's cheek. Did ghosts cry? He wasn't sure.

There was a long silence until Theo prompted again. 'Doug . . . what did she say?'

'It was the very last thing she said to me,' he whispered. 'And I *made* her say it.'

CHAPTER FIFTEEN

'You look beautiful.'

Alisha looked around to see Mum standing in the doorway, watching, as she checked out her reflection in the bedroom mirror before getting into school clothes and going down to breakfast. The white dress hung nicely on her—she seemed to have grown a little taller and leaner. 'Beautiful' was pushing it a bit—but that's what mums *had* to say. It was in their job description.

Mum stepped into the room and picked up the hairbrush. She hadn't brushed Alisha's hair since she was about six, but Alisha didn't protest as the brush gently swiped through her long dark waves. It had grown to below her shoulders over the summer term and the ends curled a little. 'So—is this what you're wearing to the disco?' Mum asked, smiling. Alisha regarded the dress, head on one side. The bodice was embroidered and high and the skirt fell in soft folds from just below the rib cage. There were tiny seed pearls stitched along the hem. It looked a little bit like a Victorian nightie—and that was perfect for the look she was going for.

'I'm going as a dead girl,' she said.

Mum winced. 'Really? Isn't that in rather poor taste?'

Alisha grinned. 'Yeah—that's the point.'

'I didn't know it was fancy dress,' said Mum.

'Well, it isn't really—but you can wear what you like so me and Kirsty and the girls decided—because it's on Friday the thirteenth—that we'd go spooky style.'

'You, Kirsty, and the girls?' Mum beamed at her.

'Yes, Mum,' said Alisha. 'That's something being on the telly got me. Friends.'

Mum looked less happy. She put down the brush and sat on Alisha's bed. 'Do you think that? Do you think that's the only reason they're including you?'

Alisha sat down too. She shrugged. 'I don't know. Probably. They only really started talking to me properly after I was on TV. And at least two of them were a bit disappointed that I didn't die and they didn't get to cry on camera . . .' She paused, thinking.

'But . . . ?' prompted Mum.

'Well . . . I've changed. I've started answering them back more.' Alisha shook her head. 'And they say they think I'm funny!'

'You *are* funny!' said Mum. 'Haven't I always said so? When you're relaxed and being yourself. So . . . what? . . . Are you saying they finally get the real you?'

'Maybe,' said Alisha. She smiled. 'Maybe *I'm* finally getting the real me. I must get struck by lightning more often!'

Mum shuddered. 'Please don't say that. Lightning never strikes twice.'

'Actually, that's not true,' said Alisha. 'Theo says there are places where lightning has struck loads of times. The Shard tower in London gets struck thirty-eight times a year on average.'

Mum put her hands over her ears and went 'Lalalalalaaaah! Can't hear you.' Then she paused, raised one eyebrow, put her hands down and said 'Theo, eh . . . ? You've been chatting to *Theo* . . . ?'

Alisha threw a pillow at her. 'Don't YOU start!'

Theo shot across the hall and vaulted over Conor as he crouched on the gym mat.

'Theo!' shouted Mr Carter. '*Wait* until people are out of the way before you take your turn!'

'Sorry, sir!' shouted Theo, tearing back around to the end of the line as his group took it in turns to leap over the vaulting horse. He loved circuit training.

After three more vaults he'd move on to scaling the gym bars and coming down the ropes. He'd always had more energy than he knew what to do with— it was why he was so fidgety. Although in the last week, he'd definitely been *less* fidgety. And better able to concentrate in class. Maybe some of his excess energy had been siphoned off by Doug and Lizzie. Maybe this was the future of treatment for ADHD— just buddy up your hyperactive kid with an energy-sucking spirit. Job done!

Everyone was barefoot and his lightning-patterned soles were no longer causing so much interest. He was relieved about that . . . and relieved that Conor and Ryan still seemed to want to be mates, even though the novelty must be wearing off. They'd all decided to go to tomorrow night's disco together. As Theo climbed the gym bars he felt a glow of happiness. Coming down south and leaving all his friends behind had been tough . . . but now he had *five* new friends. OK—so two of them were *girls*, but he wasn't sexist. And two of them were *dead*, but he wasn't ghostist either . . .

His chortle at his own joke faltered as his thoughts wandered back to Doug's visit last night. Theo had not known what to say to him about KJ, as Doug called her. He understood completely the sadness in

Karen Rathbone's eyes yesterday. He wondered if she had ever told her parents. It was all so sad . . . but he didn't know what to do about it. He didn't know how to help and, anyway, Doug had just faded away before he could think of anything to say.

Theo shook his head and climbed higher on the gym bars. Maybe Alisha would have something useful to say. He would talk to her about it as soon as he got the chance.

He was high above everyone's heads when he saw the figure at the window. He could not make out the face as it was shadowed, but the shoulders were hunched and the head was bowed, under some kind of grey hood. Theo froze on the ropes. The figure was eerie enough, but eerier still was that the windows in the school hall were high—their sills at least two metres off the ground. To look through them like this, the watcher would have to be up a ladder. And yet the figure was swaying and moving as if it were walking to and fro.

'Oi—Theo! Go on!' yelled Conor, from above. 'You're slowing us down!'

But Theo could not move. Only his eyes scanned left and right. There were six high arched windows on either side of the hall . . . and shadowy hooded figures were looking in through three of them. Theo felt a chill hit him like an avalanche of ice—and he plummeted off the ropes.

He hit the gym mat hard but in a second he was back up on his feet, staring wildly around at all the windows. The dark figures were still there. *Still there!*

Conor thumped down next to him. 'You all right?' he grunted. 'You look like you're going to chuck up.'

Theo pointed up at the windows. 'Who are *they*?'

Conor followed his eyeline and then looked back at Theo, puzzled. 'Who?'

Mr Carter arrived beside them. 'Theo? Are you feeling sick?' he demanded. 'Conor—go and get the waste paper bin.'

But Theo wasn't feeling sick. He was feeling *terrified*. He swung around to the teacher and croaked: 'Look! Up at the windows! Who *are* they?'

Mr Carter looked and when he looked back at Theo he spoke slowly and calmly. 'Theo . . . there's nobody at the windows. Did you hit your head when you fell off the ropes?'

'No!' shouted Theo. By now everyone had stopped their circuit and his whole class was staring at him. They were looking up at the windows, too, but not one of them seemed freaked out—just baffled.

'Everyone—carry on!' yelled Mr Carter. 'Conor— please go and ask Miss Phillips to drop in and take over for me. 'I'm taking Theo to the sick room.'

Theo didn't protest that he wasn't feeling sick. In a way, he was. Sick with fear. The faces at the windows were still there, following his progress as he walked unsteadily across the hall, Mr Carter holding his arm. He could not see their eyes or their expressions . . . but he *knew* they were watching him. He could *feel* it.

'Come on, Theo. Stay with me,' said Mr Carter, as Theo sagged against him and then collapsed in the corridor.

'It's red satin and I've got this black bead choker and some of that white makeup stuff, you know, from the Halloween shop and—' Kirsty stopped whispering abruptly as Mrs Gardner turned back around from the whiteboard.

Alisha grinned to herself. She'd always thought she was just fine on her own; that she didn't *need* to be in with the cool crowd to be OK. And in her heart she knew this was partly true. Your whole life could not be about trying to fit in. But, oh, it was so nice when you did. It really made life so much lighter and happier when people said hi to you in the corridor and other girls included you in the gossip. Instead of trying to shut herself up all the time, afraid of getting teased for being a 'brainbox', she was now just saying what she thought . . . well, mostly. She wasn't stupid enough to let it *all* out.

It was weird to think that two weeks ago she'd had no proper friends at all . . . and now she had *five*. Admittedly, two of them were quite old, technically. And dead. But that didn't matter. It was amazing. What would Kirsty and Sophie say if they knew she and Theo hung out with two ghost kids after school?

As Mrs Gardner started taking them through a method of long division, Alisha got a very sudden and intense need to go to the toilet. She put her hand up and asked to be excused and, somewhat impatiently, Mrs Gardner nodded her out of the room. Out in the corridor things went a bit odd. For a start, the intense need abruptly passed. But now she felt very cold. Maybe she was coming down with a bladder infection!

Then she saw the face at the window.

'Your mum's on her way,' said Mr Carter.

Theo lay on the couch in the small room behind the school reception, his knees drawn up like a baby. He was afraid to look up at the window in case another looming dark figure was looking in, but when he forced himself to glance at it, nothing swayed there but the branches of a slender sycamore tree.

Mr Carter sat on a nearby seat and gazed at Theo, concerned. 'How are you feeling? Your colour is a little better. Maybe you don't need to be sick after all.'

Theo shook his head. 'No. I'll be OK.'

'So—what exactly did you see at the windows?'

Theo shook his head again. 'I don't know,' he mumbled into the blanket rolled up under his cheek. 'I can't remember now. I think I was a bit faint.' Why was he lying? *Because he won't believe you,* he answered himself.

'Your mum said the doctor warned about the odd funny turn,' went on Mr Carter. 'A bit of brain rebooting, remember?'

Theo nodded and stared bleakly at the floor.

'You probably overdid it on the circuit training . . . maybe got a rush of blood to the brain . . . or not *enough* blood to the brain,' Mr Carter continued. 'Try not to worry about it. You'll be fine again tomorrow.'

'Sir,' said Theo, suddenly. 'Can Alisha come in here?'

Mr Carter looked surprised but he shrugged and said he'd ask Mrs Gardner.

'Don't tell Mrs Gardner what you want Alisha *for,*' added Theo. 'She'll be embarrassed.'

Leaving him under the care of the receptionist, Mr Carter went off to get Alisha to wait with Theo.

When Alisha arrived she looked very uneasy.

'Sorry,' said Theo. 'Did you get embarrassed in class when Mr Carter came to get you?'

'What? Er—no . . . no I wasn't in class. I was in the corridor,' said Alisha. She seemed distracted but she snapped back into the here and now and sat down beside him. 'What happened? Mr Carter said you fainted in PE.'

'I didn't faint,' said Theo. 'I was conscious the whole time.' He glanced at the receptionist, but she was busy on the phone. He lowered his voice anyway. 'I saw people at the window.'

Alisha blinked. 'So did I. About five minutes ago.'

Theo sat up, slightly abashed. Alisha seemed to be taking this a lot better than he was.

'Well . . . a person,' amended Alisha. 'It was Lizzie! She was peering in at me through the window over the coat pegs and waving. She looked . . . worried.'

'What did she say?' asked Theo.

'Nothing,' said Alisha. 'She just faded out. You know she can't last long when she moves away from the common. But I think we need to go and see them at lunch break, if we can get away.'

'I won't be here at lunch break!' said Theo. 'My mam's coming to get me. I'll probably have to stay in bed all afternoon.'

'Are you sick?' asked Alisha, suddenly noticing how pale he looked.

'No . . . I'm scared.' Theo rubbed his hands through his hair, making it even more stand-on-end than usual. 'Alisha . . . I saw people at the window,' he said, again.

'Yeah—so you said,' replied Alisha. 'What about it?'

'No—you don't get it. They were at the school *hall* windows. Four of them, looking in.'

Alisha frowned. 'What . . . up on a ladder or something?'

'I don't think they *need* a ladder,' said Theo. 'They were dead people.'

Alisha got the chills again. Seeing Lizzie had been startling, but not scary. Lizzie was her friend, after all—and she couldn't help it that her presence caused Alisha to rapidly cool down. What was troubling Alisha was the worry in Lizzie's face. She'd never seen Lizzie look worried.

And if Theo was seeing other dead people, maybe there was a reason for it.

'What did they look like?' she asked.

'Just shapes—shadows,' said Theo, scrunching up bits of the thin blanket he was sitting on. 'Grey hoods and dark faces in shadow.'

'Wow — regulation ghosties,' said Alisha. 'Well . . . we did see that old lady in the graveyard, didn't we? Lizzie said we'd be able to see others. Maybe we'll see lots of them from now on.' She shivered, not much liking the idea. 'They won't all be fun like Doug and Lizzie, I guess.'

'Look . . . if I'd just seen one drifting by in a regulation ghostie way, well, I'd be a bit freaked but not . . . not like this.' Theo had clenched fistfuls of blanket now and Alisha could see he was *really* scared. 'It was the way they were *watching me*. I don't know how I know that, when I couldn't see their eyes, but they *were* watching me.'

'OK — I'm going down to the hall. I'll see if *I* can see them,' said Alisha. 'How long until your mum gets here?'

Theo checked his watch. 'About ten minutes, probably.'

'OK — I'll run. I'll be back in two ticks.'

And as the corridors were empty, during lesson time, she took a risk and *did* run. She didn't clump along noisily as she would have a couple of weeks back, but sprinted lightly on the balls of her feet, making very little sound. She did not want a teacher to come out of a classroom and order her to walk . . . and then ask where she was going.

The school hall was nearly empty when she arrived, with just a few kids putting away some equipment in the cupboard. She glanced up at the windows. There were six along each side of the hall—tall and arched, allowing in plenty of light—but with high sills, way above her head. Nobody could casually wander past and peer in—unless the builders had some scaffolding up . . . that might be possible. She hadn't seen any scaffolding when she was outside, though. She stared hard at each of the twelve windows in turn but saw nothing. She didn't know whether Theo would be glad about this or not. Maybe he wanted to share the experience with her . . . or maybe he wanted to know they were gone.

Alisha turned to go—and then she saw something that made her freeze. In the corner of the hall, opposite where the kids were putting away the last few mats and balls, was a doorway which led to the caretaker's basement. The door, with its faded blue paint and black handle, was shut—but a dark grey swirl of cloud was drifting around it. At first it looked like smoke and she wondered whether she should run straight to the fire alarm and smash the glass in it . . . but part of her knew that this was *not* smoke. A couple of boys walked past after closing the PE cupboard. They chatted away as normal and neither of them mentioned the dark cloud, although they would surely have seen it had it been real. And now that she looked closely at it she could make out movement . . . as if two or three people were standing in the darkness, restlessly swaying. And tiny green sparks of light. A cold spiral of dread began to rise up through her stomach as the lower part of the shadow began to roll across the scuffed wooden floor towards her.

She ran.

CHAPTER SIXTEEN

For the second time that week, Alisha played truant. She hoped that being asked by Mr Carter to sit with Theo would cover her absence for a while, but she'd probably get caught out this time. You couldn't go missing for a whole afternoon without a teacher noticing.

But she *had* to find Lizzie and Doug. And then she had to see Theo. His mum had arrived to take him home just as she'd got back from the hall, and she hadn't been able to tell him anything about the creepy grey figures. She could only give him an urgent nod to convey that she understood and, yes, there *was* something weird in the school hall—and then he was gone and she was left alone in the corridor.

As she slipped away again to the school gates, Alisha tried hard to manage the panicky shakes radiating from her insides. Maybe creepy grey figures would drift around them all the time from now on and they'd just have to get used to it. Hey!

There might even be upsides to it, she told herself. It could be quite a useful form of air conditioning on hot stuffy days . . . just position a departed soul in a corner of your sitting room and let them suck the heat out. Perhaps a biddable poltergeist could hand her a book while she was lounging in bed on a Saturday morning. Or switch the light off for her when she was ready to sleep.

But, as she sprinted down the road with her bag bumping on her back, Alisha couldn't imagine ever getting used to this. Full colour, normal-looking characters like Doug and Lizzie were one thing . . . but dark, drifting, shapeless souls forever hanging about . . . she couldn't joke herself into liking *that* idea. She was quite happy to be a hauntee for Doug and Lizzie, but she didn't want to make friends with all the other afterlifers in the area.

She went to the tree first but couldn't raise the dead. Then she tried the graveyard, by Doug's headstone. Still nothing . . . and worse . . . she thought she caught another of those drifting greys in the corner of her eye, just under the arched gateway. Shivering, she ran back up the common to the ornamental lake and found the old dead tree which had been killed at the same time as her two seventies-throwback friends. She pushed through a clump of holly saplings and a patch of brambles and went straight to it, pressing her hands against its worn, sun-bleached trunk.

'Come *on*, Lizzie!' she whispered, leaning her forehead above her hands. 'What were you trying to tell me?'

It was Doug who showed up, standing a couple of steps away beside the clump of holly saplings. 'Lizzie can't come,' he said. 'She's all used up for today. It took all her energy to get down to your school and find you.'

'Why did she want to find me?' asked Alisha. Doug looked a bit low on energy too—he was more see-through than usual.

'She wanted to warn you,' he said, pushing his hands deep into the pockets of his flared trousers. She got a message from a sage.'

Alisha blinked. 'A sage?'

He looked uncomfortable and even more see-through. 'Some of them . . . I mean, *us* . . . some of us can see stuff coming. Or they say they can. We call them sages. This sage . . . he warned Lizzie there was something coming. Something dark. With flashes.'

'What . . . like lightning? Are we going to get struck again?' Alisha gulped, remembering her comment to Mum first thing that day, about lightning striking twice.

'No—not lightning. Flashing lights,' said Doug.

'She said the sage showed her flashing lights and darkness . . . at your school.'

Alisha thought for a moment and then relaxed. 'Oh! Well, the school disco is tomorrow night. There should be loads of flashing lights in the dark.'

'She saw pale faces, too. Children looking pale and ill.'

'Um, yeah,' said Alisha, feeling slightly embarrassed. 'Me and some friends, we're going spooky style . . . with white makeup.'

'Oh . . . right,' said Doug. 'Well . . . that's OK then. It wouldn't be the first time a sage has got worked up over nothing. Some of them are so old they think a digital watch is dark magic. I'll tell Lizzie to cool the "jeepers" action.'

'Is she really all used up for today?' asked Alisha, disappointed. 'Can't she use some of my energy?'

'Nah,' said Doug. 'You haven't got enough. Did you eat any lunch today?' He sounded like a concerned parent.

'No—not yet,' said Alisha. 'I had to get out of school to find out what was happening with you two. And there's been weird stuff going on, Dougie. Theo saw ghosts today, peering through the hall windows. He was really scared. And . . . I saw something grey and swirly in the corner of the hall.'

Doug shrugged. 'We did say you might see some others. They're probably just curious. I wouldn't worry.'

'But . . . it's . . . creepy!' said Alisha.

'They can't *help* it,' said Doug, looking slightly offended. 'The older ones kind of go pale over time. It's hard to keep yourself all coloured-in after centuries of haunting. It takes energy. That's why there are so many grey ladies. They don't want to be grey any more than my gran did when she used to buy hair dye and put on make-up. But you can't get spirit dye or ghost blusher . . .'

Alisha smiled, imagining pale spirits trying to brush some colour into their cheeks. 'Look—I'm not judging them. I just got scared. Can you ask them to leave us alone . . . ?'

Doug shook his head. 'I don't know who they were so I can't ask them anything. But I'll see what I can find out. Don't worry about it. They can't hurt you.' He grinned, suddenly. 'They're probably more afraid of you than you are of them . . .'

'Oh—right,' said Alisha. 'So maybe I could just trap them under a glass, slide a bit of paper underneath, and release them back into the spirit world!' Doug laughed and she giggled, feeling a little better.

'Come back tomorrow,' said Doug, fading fast

now. 'Lizzie should be all juiced up again by then. Can you bring an iPad? I want to see if we can pick up *Doctor Who* on iPlayer . . .'

'I haven't *got* an iPad!' said Alisha, but Doug had gone. She let out a long sigh. Doug seemed pretty unbothered about all the ghostly goings on at school. So why should she worry about it? He was right. Those spirits couldn't help looking all sinister and shadowy. They were probably just trying to be friendly, like Doug and Lizzie, but didn't have enough energy to be properly seen or heard. She should feel sorry for them, really. Give them a smile and a wave, next time. She would go and see Theo, now, and tell him the same.

It was just a matter of getting used to it. That was all.

As she refocused on the here and now, she noticed two people standing over on the other side of the lake. It was Sophie—with what looked like Sophie's mum. Alisha suddenly remembered that Sophie had gone off for a dental appointment that morning—she must be on her way back to school. Except that she wasn't going anywhere. She was just staring at Alisha while her mum was asking her something and glancing across anxiously.

Alisha suddenly realized, with a dropping

sensation in her stomach, that they had been watching her while she was talking to Doug. She must have looked completely barmy—like she was in earnest conversation with a bunch of holly saplings. Alisha drew a deep breath and then smiled and gave them a little wave. She had absolutely *no idea* how to explain this.

'Are you OK, love?' called Sophie's mum. 'Do you need help?'

Alisha walked briskly away from the holly clump and along the path on the other side of the lake. 'I'm fine!' she called. 'Just going for a doctor's check-up! Meeting Mum down there . . .' She waved vaguely in the direction of the other end of the common, where people parked cars to take their dogs for a walk.

'Are you sure . . . ?' Sophie's mum called after her.

'Yeah—see you tomorrow, Sophie!' called Alisha, speeding up. She was so embarrassed, they might be able to see the bright red glow of her face even from across the lake. Thankfully they just walked on, with the occasional glance back, and were soon out of sight. And then what? The minute they got into school she would be found out. The school would call home, wondering what she was doing on the common, talking to invisible people, when she should be in class. Mum would be worried and angry.

And hey . . . so much for being accepted by the cool girls.

What could she tell Kirsty? That she had been reciting an audition speech from a play? On her own under a dead tree? That she had suddenly got a phone with a hands-free kit and was talking to her mum? That Sophie and her mother had just gone mad and made it all up?

No. It was all over. She was back on the outside again.

CHAPTER SEVENTEEN

There was a glowing light at the end of a dark tunnel. A deep, kind voice, emanated from it.

'Run, Theo! Run to the light!'

Theo felt slightly hysterical but then he realized the voice was *actually* saying, 'Come on, Theo. Look into the light.'

Dr Karish peered into the ophthalmoscope and then clicked it off. 'Well, your eyes look normal enough and all your vital signs are as they should be,' he said, returning the eye-inspection gadget to his black case.

'Are you sure there's nothing amiss?' asked Mam, hovering behind Theo and patting his hair. 'I mean . . . to drop off the ropes like that and then pass out . . . it's worrying.'

'Well, I'm fairly sure it's just a bit of delayed brain rebooting, as I explained to you in the hospital,' said the doctor. 'But to be on the safe side I will get him in for an MRI scan as soon as possible. Although he did have one while he was admitted last time and nothing untoward showed up. Seems reasonable to have another look, though. Even if the images are normal, which is what I'd expect, at least it will set your mind at rest. It will probably take a day or two to set it up.'

'Thank you,' said Mam. 'I would appreciate that. So . . . in the meantime, should I send him back to school tomorrow?'

'If he feels up to it, certainly,' said Dr Karish.

'I *do* feel up to it,' said Theo. 'I feel fine now! I could even go back today.' Theo realized that getting away to see Alisha, Doug, and Lizzie was going to be difficult now. He wished he'd toughed it out at school and not let them call Mam.

'You're going nowhere other than the settee for the rest of today!' said Mam. 'And you're going to get some REST!'

Theo knew he must convince her he was fine by the end of the evening. Tomorrow was the school disco day and there was no way he was missing that. But more importantly, he *had* to catch up with Alisha and find out what she'd seen in the school hall. Her expression had said she was right there with him in Weirdsville. And *she* had managed not to have a girly faint about it. Theo was beginning to feel quite annoyed at the number of times he'd swooned recently when Alisha had stayed conscious.

As it turned out, he didn't have to wait until the next day. Only minutes after Dr Karish had left there was a knock at the door and Alisha was outside. Theo was on the settee by this time and able to peer down the hall as Mam opened the door.

'Oh—hello, Alisha,' she said, warmly. 'Have you come to check on Theo? Come on in, love.'

Alisha came in, smiling but looking worried. 'I think I've done a stupid thing,' she said. 'I left school too early. But I was really worried and . . . well . . . would you mind calling my mum and letting her know I'm here with Theo? I don't want her to get a call from the school and then get all worried because I've not gone home.'

'Oh dear—you two are in a state today!' said Theo's mum. 'OK—I'll call your mam now, flower, and she can let the school know. To be honest, I'm wondering whether either of you really should have gone back so soon.'

Once his mam had gone off to make the call, Alisha sat down next to Theo with a bump. 'You're right. There's something weird haunting the hall. I saw it.' She told Theo what she had witnessed swirling out from the caretaker's door.

'I went to the common but I couldn't get Lizzie to show up,' she said. 'Only Doug. He said she was trying to get hold of me at the school to warn me. That's why I saw her through the window.'

'Warn you?' Theo sat up straight and shoved away the fleecy blanket Mam had deposited on him. 'About what? The grey ghosts?'

'No . . .' Alisha shrugged. 'About something else. Flashing lights on disco night!' She snorted. 'Apparently some other ghost showed her flashing lights in our future—tomorrow night. And pale, ill-looking kids. I told Doug we were having a disco . . . and that me and Kirsty, and Sophie, and the others are going as ghosts and vampires and so on.'

Theo wrinkled his brow. 'You are? Why?!'

'Because tomorrow is Friday the thirteenth!' said Alisha. 'Kirsty says it's always good to theme your look. So we're theming it spooky style!'

'OK . . . if that's what makes you happy,' said Theo, with a shrug.

'Well, it probably won't make me happy now,' said Alisha, her shoulders suddenly slumping.

'What . . . you and all the cool girls, hanging out looking like the brides of Dracula?'

She clicked her teeth. 'Yeah, that'll be brilliant . . .

right up to the point when Sophie tells them that I talk to myself.'

Theo peered at her, puzzled. 'What *are* you mithering about?'

Alisha dropped her face into her hands and let out a groan. 'Just as I was talking to Doug, up by their old lightning tree, Sophie and her mum walked by. They were watching me the whole time! They think I'm a total freak!'

'Are you sure they saw you?'

'Yes! They called over to ask me if I was all right! And why wouldn't they? I was standing there rabbiting away to a *clump of holly*!'

'Ah,' said Theo. He understood now. Being caught out chatting to invisible people was never good for your reputation at school. No wonder Alisha looked so horror-struck.

'Maybe Sophie will just keep it to herself . . . ?' he offered, with a feeble grin.

'Yeah—and maybe Mr Carter will come to school tomorrow in high heels and a frilly miniskirt,' said Alisha.

'That probably *is* more likely,' admitted Theo. 'So . . . tell them you were rehearsing for a play or something! Or on a call on your mobile . . . hands free.'

'I haven't got a mobile . . . and I have never been in a play!' said Alisha.

'It's never too late . . . tell them the lightning strike brought out your inner luvvie! Anyway,' went on Theo, in a lower voice. 'There was something else I wanted to tell you about . . . something that happened last night—'

'Alisha—your mum wants you to go straight home,' said Theo's mum, coming in at that moment and giving her a sympathetic smile. 'It's OK. I don't think you're in big trouble but you need to get going.'

'OK,' said Alisha, getting up and picking up her school bag and shrugging at Theo. His other news would have to wait now. 'Thanks for calling her, Mrs Rooney. I'll see you tomorrow, Theo. Won't I?'

'Yes!' said Theo.

'We'll see how you are in the morning,' said Mam, patting his head.

'I'll be *fine*. See you at school, Alisha—thanks for visiting.'

Alisha trooped home slowly, not keen to have a chat with Mum about her odd behaviour. It was still a few minutes before the end of school, so at least she wouldn't have to worry about bumping into Kirsty and Sophie. She shuddered as she imagined Sophie telling Kirsty all about that weirdo, Alisha, alone on the common, talking to herself. And probably Sophie's mum had done the same with the school receptionist and it was all over the staffroom by now, too. Mum was probably already booking the appointment with a child psychiatrist . . .

She paused on the pavement as a builder's truck pulled up sharply to the kerb. A man in a fluorescent yellow vest jumped out of the passenger side, ran to a nearby privet hedge, and threw up in it. Alisha stood still, clutching the straps of her school bag tightly, not sure whether to walk on by or ask him if he needed help. Seriously. Could today get any stranger?

But the man's colleague jumped out of the driver's side and came round to check on him before she could speak. 'Whoa—better out than in, mate!' she heard him say as he patted his colleague on the shoulder. He looked vaguely familiar . . . and she realized suddenly that he and his nauseous mate were a couple of the builders who were working on the library extension back at school. 'Had a bad curry for breakfast or something?' the driver queried. 'Chris . . . ? Are you OK?' he added, sounding less jocular as his workmate sank into the hedge, shivering.

'I don't know,' said Chris.

'Um . . . do you need me to get help?' asked Alisha, nervously.

They both looked up at her in surprise.

'Nah,' said the driver, an older man than Chris, with a weather-beaten face and grey hair. 'He'll be all right. I'll get him home to bed. Thanks, sweetheart. You get on now. Don't breathe in, eh?' he chuckled, wafting the air in front of his face and wrinkling his nose.

Chris tried to smile too, but he looked awful, thought Alisha. Pale and almost grey. As the other man tried to haul him to his feet by the upper arm, he let out a yelp of pain.

'What? What is it?' asked his workmate.

'Just—really sore,' muttered Chris, cupping his shoulder with one hand. But he got up and back into the truck and they drove away. Alisha walked past the hedge holding her nose and not looking. It was time to get home. She'd really had enough of today . . .

CHAPTER EIGHTEEN

'I was saying a prayer,' said Alisha.

Kirsty and Sophie stared at her. 'A . . . prayer?' echoed Kirsty, looking as if she might burst at any moment. With hysterical laughter. Alisha knew she had to play it straight now . . . to appeal to Kirsty's over-developed sense of drama.

'Look . . . I can tell you the whole story, but not if you're just going to laugh,' she said. 'I don't expect anyone else will understand, either. Even my mum thought I was bonkers.'

Kirsty and Sophie looked at each other. Nearby the other girls hovered, waiting to find out what their leader was getting from Alisha after half a morning of sniggering and finger pointing.

Alisha glanced across at them and then back at Kirsty, holding the girl's gaze. 'I won't tell *them*,' she said. 'But . . . if you think you can listen without going into hysterics, I might tell you.'

Kirsty and Sophie exchanged glances. On the one

hand, the fun to be had out of the whole 'Alisha going nuts' routine could be astronomical. It would last the rest of term . . . no . . . the rest of Alisha's school life! But . . . on the other hand, being let in on a secret was pretty irresistible too.

'Don't worry,' said Alisha, gathering up her school bag from the playground wall. 'I won't hang around with you all at the disco tonight if you don't want me to. I know you think I'm a weirdo. Maybe I am. See you.' And she walked away three steps before Kirsty called her back.

'Alisha . . . we *don't* think you're a weirdo,' she said. 'And . . . saying a prayer . . . that's a sweet thing to do. You can trust us. Tell us.'

Alisha paused and then turned back slowly. 'Did you know that there were some other kids . . .' she said, '. . . who were killed on the common by lightning?'

'No. Who? When?' asked Kirsty, agog.

'A long time ago,' said Alisha. 'Back in the 1970s. I've been doing a bit of research. The tree you saw me standing next to, Sophie—two kids, a bit older than us, were killed there in the summer of 1976. Elizabeth Holt and Douglas Crane. They died instantly.'

Kirsty and Sophie were looking genuinely

intrigued now. 'Really? How do you know?' asked Kirsty.

'I did—well, to be honest, *Theo* did—a bit of research at the *Echo* office. The reporter who interviewed us helped him.'

That was a good call. As soon as she mentioned the press, Kirsty and Sophie perked up even more. 'So,' she went on, 'I read the cuttings and . . . I don't know . . . I felt really, really sad about it yesterday. I suddenly *had* to go and find the tree. And so I did. I bunked off lessons and I went and while I was there I just . . . sort of said a prayer to them. I know that's weird but . . .'

'No,' said Kirsty. 'That's not weird. We understand, don't we?' Sophie nodded vigorously. 'You've been through *such* a lot,' went on Kirsty, patting Alisha's shoulder. 'We'll keep a close eye on you and make sure you're OK. And you must definitely come to the disco tonight! It wouldn't be the same without you.'

And they both walked back to the others in silence. And then there was a burst of giggles as the bell went.

Alisha sighed and walked back into class.

'Page sixteen. Feudalism in the fourteenth century!' said Mr Carter.

There was a groan around the class, but as the lesson got underway it wasn't all that bad. Theo was realizing he liked history quite a lot. It tickled him to think that Mr Carter might be right and he might have a bit of a feel for the subject. Not one of his teachers in Rotherham had ever said he had a feel for anything—except mayhem. He found himself reading ahead in the textbook and flicking through pages of pictures—old etchings of maps, richly coloured oil paintings of lords and ladies and muddy-looking watercolours of downtrodden farm labourers.

He became so absorbed that he didn't hear Mr Carter the first time. It must have been the second or third time that the teacher addressed him that he finally looked up, because by then the whole class was staring at him. 'Sorry! Sorry, sir,' said Theo. 'I was . . . reading.'

Mr Carter sighed. 'So then, this time you'll know all about the reasons for the peasant uprisings against the land owners, won't you, Theo. Please enlighten us!'

Theo gulped. What *did* he know? There was a long pause and then he opened his mouth. 'It was the plagues,' he said. 'Plagues wiped out so many of them that those who were left started haggling, you know? For decent pay for their work. It's supply and demand, isn't it? People started getting bolder. You would, wouldn't you? Especially if you thought you might be dead next week anyway—what would you have to lose?'

Once again, Mr Carter looked impressed. He nodded and said 'You're right, Theo. In the 1300s the plague carried off anything from a third to two thirds of the people in the country. Nobody's quite sure how many because the record keeping wasn't great back then . . .' He went on for a while longer but Theo wasn't listening. His ears seemed to be blocked. And his throat suddenly felt painful, as if his tonsils had abruptly swollen up. Alarmed, he put his hands to his neck but couldn't feel any lumps with his fingertips. But now his joints ached and there were shooting pains in his armpits.

He glanced around at his classmates but nobody seemed to have noticed that he was screwing up his face with pain. Well . . . nobody except the figure at the window . . . a dark, hooded figure with indistinguishable features. Theo felt a deep chill fighting with the feverish heat now pounding through him. He wanted to jump up and demand that everyone look at the figure at the window. *LOOK! LOOK! It's here again! It's here NOW!*

But if he did this there was no way he would avoid being carted off to the hospital for a brain scan and an emergency appointment with the child psychiatry department. And he was NOT mad! There really WAS a figure at the window!

Theo closed his eyes and tried to take long, slow breaths as a wave of nausea hit him. Mr Carter had his back to the class now, writing something on the board, and was talking animatedly. He couldn't see how ill Theo must now surely look. Theo's heart was racing with panic. His armpits really, really HURT.

And then there was a CRASH and suddenly a chunk of stone was in the middle of Theo's desk.

A thin cloud of dust rose from it as his pencils and pens scattered and rolled off on to the floor with small rattles and pings. Theo sat staring at the chunk of stone, amazed. He looked up, expecting to see a hole in the ceiling where the stone had fallen through, but the ceiling looked just the same as usual.

'Theo—what on EARTH is that?!' demanded Mr Carter. So at least Theo knew the stone was *real* and he wasn't hallucinating *that*. He glanced at the window and saw the figure was gone. And so were his symptoms. Apart from the receding fear and shock, he was almost normal. No pain or nausea or feverishness; just his poor brain trying to bend itself around exactly *how* a lump of stone was sitting on his desk.

'I-I don't know, sir,' he croaked as Mr Carter marched up to him. The teacher stared at the stone and then said: 'Oh—I see! You've found another bit!'

Stunned, Theo peered at the stone and realized that there was writing engraved on it. It was in the same style as the writing on the stone that Chris, the builder, had brought in to show Mr Carter earlier that week. More Latin. Mr Carter picked it up and examined it closely. 'Must have been heavy in your bag,' he observed. 'Where did you find it?'

'Um . . .' Theo couldn't think of what to say. His hyperactive brain seemed to have gone to sleep. 'Um . . . just . . . around here,' he finished, lamely. Where *had* it come from? Thin air?! Had it literally arrived from some other dimension? Maybe Doug and Lizzie were messing around with him . . . but no. They had said quite clearly that they couldn't do anything more than blow air around and give people the chills—and it would take quite some puff to move a chunk of stone!

But Mr Carter wasn't listening anyway. He was walking back down to his desk where the other chunk of stone lay, wrapped in a plastic bag. He unwrapped it and put the two side by side. They fitted roughly together. Theo went to the desk and saw the new chunk of stone had STILENC engraved on it. 'Can you read it now?' he asked in a low voice. The class had subsided into general chatter behind them.

Mr Carter frowned and ran his fingers along the worn old engraving. 'Ever open for . . .' he said. 'And then . . . something else . . . *est* . . . something . . . and *stilenc* . . . It's still too incomplete. I'll need to study it properly. Strange. I wonder if the builders have found any more.'

'You could ask Chris,' suggested Theo.

'I would, but he's not in today. Off sick, according to the site foreman I was chatting to earlier. So . . . well done, Theo. Good find.'

Theo nodded and touched the stone lightly. Sure enough a chill shot up through his hand and lower arm as if he'd just dunked his fingers into a deep freeze. It was connected. This stone, the Latin, the faces at the windows . . . he had to tell Alisha at lunchtime. They must get back to the common to find Doug and Lizzie straight after school. Surely their ghostly friends would have *some* idea what this was all about.

He just hoped there wouldn't be any more weird stuff until then. He really didn't think he could take much more . . .

CHAPTER NINETEEN

The little girl stood in the corner of the classroom as if she'd been naughty. And maybe she had been but, frankly, she had bigger problems to deal with.

For a start, there was her face. Her features were chalky pale, but there was black on the end of her nose, around her mouth, and at the point of her small chin, as if she'd had her face too close to a bonfire. Her hair, scraped back into some kind of thin cotton cap, revealed small, blackened ears. Her eyes were swollen almost shut.

Breathe, breathe . . . just breathe, Alisha told herself. *It's OK. It's fine. She's just saying hello.*

Emma walked to the front of the class and got a pencil from the box on the shelf. Her hand went right through the small girl's head but she didn't seem to notice anything odd. Although maybe she shivered just a little as she walked back to her desk.

Blackened Ghost Girl had been haunting her for at least ten minutes, and Alisha didn't like it any better now than she had ten minutes ago. It had started with the chill across her neck as she worked on some sums, making her glance up at the apparition. After the first jolt of shock, she had at least managed not to scream or gasp or do anything to attract attention to herself—but all the same, her heart just kept zipping along at double speed. She wished Theo was in her class so she could share this with someone. Not that she'd wish it on anyone. The girl was clearly as she had been at death's door. Her thin body was wrapped up in some kind of shawl and her feet were bare. The toes were blackened too. Maybe she'd died in a fire. There was no colour in her so Alisha guessed she must be quite an old ghost, according to what Doug had told her. Seriously, she was going to have to get Doug and Lizzie to have a word with all these spirits and ask them to stop stalking her. She really didn't need this, especially today. There had been more giggles and funny looks from Kirsty's lot all morning, and if she showed herself up again by reacting to Blackened Ghost Girl it was going to get even worse.

It would be easier if she could at least *talk* to the apparition and ask what it wanted. If the little girl talked back she wouldn't be so scary. Because she *was* scary. Even more scary than the nameless grey swirly thing by the caretaker's door yesterday. She looked like something out of a horror film. WHAT DO YOU WANT?! Alisha asked, mentally, staring hard at the ghost. But it just continued to wait in the corner, its poor swollen eyes fixed upon her.

At last the bell rang for lunch break. She hung back as everyone left, Kirsty and her girls glancing over, still smothering giggles and comments. Maybe she could talk to the ghost once they were gone.

But by the time the others had filed out into the corridor, the apparition had faded away.

'Is everything all right, Alisha?' asked Mrs Gardner, pausing at the door. 'You look a bit pale.'

'Oh—no, I'm fine,' said Alisha, smiling. 'I just get a bit tired sometimes. Still getting back to normal.' She didn't need to add much more. There had been *a discussion* between the headteacher and her mum about the skipping off school yesterday. The head had said he would make allowances this time, but on no account was it to happen again. Mrs Gardner had been present too, looking concerned.

'Well, take it easy over lunch,' advised Mrs Gardner. 'And do make sure you eat enough food. You're looking quite skinny these days!'

So would you, thought Alisha, *if all your calories were being used up by energy-sucking ghosts*!

As she headed for the dining hall, she was torn. She

desperately wanted to find Theo and tell him what she'd seen . . . but she also really wanted to catch up with Kirsty and the others. She could sit down with them at lunch and listen to comforting, normal girly chatter about the disco tonight—check that she was still accepted, even if they *were* laughing at her. Maybe they did all think she was weird but perhaps that wasn't so bad. She could be the eccentric one in their group. They'd tease her but they'd still include her.

If she went straight off to speak to Theo—especially *in front* of them—the teasing would get far worse and then maybe she'd blow it totally. Alisha hovered at the end of the lunch queue, holding a plastic tray. Kirsty and her group had already collected their food and were settling at one of the big tables. There was one seat still free. It could be her seat . . . couldn't it?

Then she saw Theo come in. And the look on his face made the decision for her. He looked *terrible*. And she knew, right away, that he'd been seeing more ghosts too. She put the tray back and walked past Kirsty's table, with its empty seat beckoning, and straight across to Theo. As he saw her approach he didn't even speak; he just turned around and went back into the corridor. Alisha followed.

'What happened to *you* then?' she asked, as they

settled on a bench in the small courtyard area outside the dining hall.

'Another dark figure,' muttered Theo. 'And then I felt like death—really sick and ill. And then a lump of rock landed on my desk.'

'A lump of rock?' Alisha gasped. 'Who threw that?'

'Nobody in my class,' said Theo. 'It literally dropped in from nowhere!' He told her the whole story.

'Take me back to your class,' said Alisha. 'Let me see it.'

On the way she told him about Blackened Ghost Girl.

'This is getting worse, isn't it?' said Theo. 'I mean . . . seeing some grey lady by a gravestone is one thing—but when they're following us around school in broad daylight! That's just *wrong*! Ghosts aren't supposed to show up in the middle of maths, are they?'

'And they're not supposed to physically harm people, either,' said Alisha. 'But they've been making you feel really ill . . . and that rock could have hit you on the head!'

And here it was. Mr Carter wasn't there so Theo unwrapped the two chunks of stone from the plastic bag and showed them to Alisha. She couldn't work out the lettering at all (she didn't do Latin!) but as soon as she touched the stone she felt an intense coldness flow up her arms and spread right through her ribcage. Shuddering, she snatched her fingers away.

'What does it all *mean*?' she asked Theo. 'What are they trying to tell us? Are they warning us off or something, like in *Scooby-Doo*?'

'This doesn't feel too "jeepers" to me,' grunted Theo, wrapping the stones up again. 'It feels really horrible.'

'OK—so we go straight to Doug and Lizzie as soon as school is over?' said Alisha.

'Yeah,' said Theo. He kept glancing up at the windows, nervously. 'As soon as the bell goes. I wish we could go now. Just staying in here is making my skin crawl.' He gulped.

'Come on! Rub your face!' said Alisha. 'Get some colour into it! And eat some lunch. If you go all pale and faint-y again you'll get carted home and your mum won't let you out for a week. You need to hold it together so we can get to Doug and Lizzie and ask for help.'

Theo nodded. 'You're right,' he said. 'And they'll want us all caloried-up so they can use our energy.

Come on.' He took a deep breath and stared at the window. 'Shove off!' he called to it. 'I'm getting some CHIPS!'

Alisha patted his shoulder. 'Has there been one there the whole time?'

'Yup,' said Theo, and now that she had made contact with him she saw it too. A dark figure, staring in. She stepped towards it, scared to see it better, but compelled to find out whether it was a male or a female, young or old . . .

Theo grabbed her arm, though. 'No,' he said. 'Not now. Or you might end up fainting too. Come ON. Back to the dining room. It's chips day and we're going to stuff our faces!'

CHAPTER TWENTY

'No—no—no! Up! Go UP! Aaaaaw! Useless!' Doug snorted, sending a blast of spirit air onto the back of the teenage gamer's neck and making him rub it absently with one hand as he continued to pound the keypad of his smartphone with the other.

'Leave the poor boy alone,' said Lizzie, sitting up in a nearby tree above a couple of girls. 'He can't help being rubbish at Asteroid Nemesis IV. I don't remember *you* ever getting a high score on Pong!'

'Well, I never got the chance!' protested Doug. 'And anyway, who are *you* to talk, earwigging on people's private conversation?'

'She's got boyfriend trouble,' said Lizzie, peering down on the shiny straightened hair of the two girls on the grass. 'He keeps blowing hot and cold. A bit like you.' She giggled. 'Dump him!' she called down to the stricken girlfriend. 'He's a loser!'

'I should just dump him!' said the dark-haired girl, sniffing into a bit of screwed up tissue.

'Yeah,' said her auburn-haired friend. 'He's a loser.'

'Well, thank you!' said Lizzie. 'It's nice when people take notice of my wise words.'

'Oooh—have you got some suggestibles?' asked Doug. 'Cool! Let me!' He climbed up beside her on the branch, leant over and called down: 'But then again—maybe he *really loves* you but is just too shy to let you know!'

'I don't know,' said the first girl. 'He could just be shy . . .'

Doug grinned. 'I *love* suggestibles!' He and Lizzie had found that although the living were mostly very dense and unaware of the spirit world, a few—especially teenagers—were surprisingly open to suggestion.

'These two are *really* good,' said Lizzie. 'Watch this.' She hung down from the tree by her hands and then dropped to the grass beside them. 'Go and get an ice cream!' she told them. 'You really NEED an ice cream!'

'Some guys just don't know how to express themselves,' girl number two was saying. 'Maybe if you sat down and really talked . . . You know what? I think we need some ice cream!' And they got up and ambled away towards the little van beside the kids' play area.

'I'm on FIRE today!' said Lizzie, spinning round and punching the air.

'Hmmm,' said Doug. 'But suggesting ice cream to two girls on a hot day—near an ice-cream van—that's not a big challenge, is it? Suggest they go home and tidy their rooms. Let's see how far you get with that!'

But Lizzie wasn't listening, she was suddenly up on the tree branch again and peering hard across the common. 'It's Alisha and Theo,' she said. 'And . . . oh my! They've got company!'

Doug followed her gaze and let out a low whistle. The other two members of Strike Club were running across the grass—and in their wake were at least a dozen dark spirits. Mostly grey, with only occasional glimmers of colour, they rose and surged out of the ground like a tidal wave. They weren't chasing Alisha and Theo so much as keeping pace with them.

As soon as the bell had gone Alisha and Theo sped through school, meeting each other as they reached the playground gates—and then they just kept on running.

'More dead people!' Alisha gasped, as their feet pounded the pavement. 'Three more! Two in class and one in the girls' toilet. All sick and burnt-looking! One of them kept pointing to his armpit like he was trying out a new deodorant and wanted my opinion! FREAK!' She laughed, close to hysteria. 'How about you?' she puffed.

'Every window . . .' puffed back Theo. 'Jam-packed with 'em. Faceless loomy things. I'm going to call them FLTs for short.'

He was doing well, thought Alisha. They both were, considering how scary this was. They'd gone back into the school dining hall, got a big plate of chips each, and then stuffed them all, with plenty of ketchup. Kirsty and her girls had gone by then so Alisha didn't have to worry about what they might think. The food did help and it was just as well, because the next couple of hours weren't any easier.

'Look! I can see Lizzie and Doug!' said Theo, slowing down and glancing back at Alisha. He gave a shout of fear. Behind Alisha was a mob of FLTs, rising up like a cloud as he came to a halt.

Alisha looked too and began to stumble away, backwards. 'Lizzie! Doug! Heeeelp!' she wailed.

'OK—cool it!' said Doug, suddenly at her side. But he wasn't talking to her—he was addressing the mob of FLTs. They slowed down and, as they did so, Alisha and Theo could make out more form—more individual shapes among the dark cloud. There were men and women, old people and children.

'It's OK,' said Lizzie, now beside Doug. 'They can't hurt you.'

'No?' croaked Theo. 'Well they had a good try! One of them chucked a lump of stone at me!'

Doug and Lizzie exchanged serious looks. 'Really?' said Doug. 'Are you sure?'

'Yess!' hissed Theo. 'It could have brained me! Or broken my fingers!'

Lizzie was looking at Doug again. Her face was grave. 'He's got a poltergeist?' she said. 'Wow! Serious!'

'What's going *on*?' whimpered Alisha, as the dark figures stood, swaying, some of the more vivid ones fixing dim, washed-out eyes on them. 'What do they want? Did they all get killed in a fire at the school or something? I saw some of them more clearly in class and in the toilets. They looked . . . burnt at the edges!'

'Are they trying to suck up our energy?' added Theo. 'They made me feel so sick and ill today!'

'No,' said Doug, quietly. He looked deep into the crowd for a few seconds and then back at Theo and Alisha. 'They don't want to hurt you. They want to protect you.'

'From *what*?' demanded Alisha, sounding a little bit shriek-y. Well—she *felt* a little bit shriek-y.

'I'm not sure,' said Doug. 'Stay here—I'll go and talk to them.'

'Sit down,' advised Lizzie. 'Catch your breath. Don't worry—they won't come any closer. They really don't want to hurt you.'

Alisha and Theo sank on to the grass, trembling, and Lizzie knelt down in between them, madly twirling her rope beads as she watched Doug walk into the cloud of FLTs. He seemed to be absorbed by them, his shape dissipating, until he was just a blur of colour against their darkness.

'They won't . . . hurt him? Will they?' whispered Alisha.

'Noooo!' said Lizzie. But she didn't sound too sure.

'You don't sound too sure,' said Theo.

'No—I mean—it's all about energy,' said Lizzie. 'It's not like we can throw punches or anything, but some spirits can really bring your energy levels down—especially the very old ones who have little energy left for themselves and have to siphon off loads from others. They won't hurt Doug but he'll probably be a bit see-through for a while. And to be honest, with that shirt of his, it's probably a blessing!'

At last Doug returned and Lizzie was right—he *was* see-through. He looked serious too. He sat down on the grass with them and behind him the crowd of dark spirits loomed and shifted like a billowing cloud of smoke, but came no closer.

'They're telling me about a big . . . upset . . . at your school,' said Doug. 'Something is really wrong. Has anything happened there recently? Some kind of accident or . . . disruption . . . ? Something out of the ordinary?'

Alisha and Doug looked at each other, shrugging.

'Come on,' said Lizzie. 'Something must be different! What's going on there now which wasn't going on a month ago?'

'Oh—well—there's some building work going on,' said Alisha. 'They only started that a couple of weeks ago, while me and Theo were still in hospital.'

'Bingo!' said Lizzie. 'That'll be it! Building work . . . digging and demolishing . . . that can really mess with the spirit world sometimes. What have they done so far?'

'Not much,' said Theo. 'They've only dug the footings . . . and they didn't demolish anything beforehand. They're using up a bit of the school field to build the new library.'

'What did they tell you?' Alisha asked Doug. 'Surely *they* can explain what's up?'

'Well they could, maybe, if they weren't so old and

faded and Middle-English!' said Doug, with a sigh. 'They spent huge amounts of energy following you from the school—look, they're fading away now.' True enough, the army of FLTs was beginning to look more like a light mist now than a dark cloud. 'And even the strongest one was very faint,' went on Doug. 'All he could do was quote Chaucer at me!'

'Chaucer?' Theo looked tired and confused.

'Chaucer was a poet in the fourteenth century,' explained Lizzie. 'We studied him at school. He wrote *The Canterbury Tales*. It was all written in Middle English—a very early kind of English . . . different from what we speak now. So what *did* your olde worlde buddy manage to say, Doug?'

Doug drew his brows together as he tried to deliver the lines correctly: 'Privee theef men clepeth Deeth,' he said.

'And you recognized that as Chaucer?!' said Lizzie, looking astounded. 'Doug—I never knew you studied so hard in English!'

'I didn't,' admitted Doug. 'The guy said "CHAUCER" quite clearly and then that line.'

'Seriously, though . . . ?' said Alisha, feeling a burst of frustration. 'He couldn't just tell you *what's wrong*?!'

'Not without modern language, no,' said Doug.

'They all tried though, with pictures; people looking all pale and blackened round the edges, like they were caught in a fire. Maybe there was a fire in your school's history and they're worried it'll happen again. That could be why they're haunting you. Did your school burn down in the past?'

Again, Alisha and Theo had to shrug. 'But we can find out,' said Theo. 'The *Echo* office librarian was really helpful when I went to look up stuff about you two . . .'

'Oooh! That photo!' said Lizzie, wincing. 'They had to use the *worst* school photo I *ever* had taken!'

'Erm . . . a little focus, Liz?' said Doug. 'Major hauntee freak-out going on here!'

'Anyway,' went on Theo. 'We could go back there today and ask for any cuttings they have on Beechwood Junior School. See what we can find.'

'Good idea,' said Doug.

'Do you think that's it, Lizzie?' asked Alisha. 'That there's going to be a fire? That would be light flashing in the dark wouldn't it? Like your sage showed you.'

Lizzie screwed up her face. 'It didn't look like fire. The flashes were more blue and green than yellow.' She shook her head. 'Sorry—I can't be sure what he was on about. But . . . maybe you shouldn't go to the disco tonight, to be on the safe side.'

'No way,' said Theo. 'If something's going to happen, we should be there to warn people.'

Lizzie nodded. 'OK—so do your research; check out the school history. It might give us some answers. Should I go with them now, Doug? Do you think I'd last that far?'

Doug shook his head. 'No—we should both go back to the school with them tonight. And I'm really fading out here.' It was true—Alisha could clearly see the trees and grass through Doug's head now. 'So . . . Lizzie and me . . . we'll scoot around the common and try to pick up some energy from that lot.' He waved towards some kids and parents arriving in the sunny play area near the ice-cream van. 'When are you going to go back to school?'

'The disco starts at 6.30,' said Alisha. 'And I've got to go over to Kirsty's house and get ready with the girls.' She felt a pang of worry about whether she was still welcome—but disregarded it. Now was not the time to stress about her popularity. 'So if we go to the *Echo* right now, we should have time.'

'Won't your mam have a fit if you don't get home soon?' asked Theo. 'Especially after yesterday . . . ?'

'No—she won't be back from work until 4.30, and Dad's not back until about six,' said Alisha. 'We've just got time. How about yours?'

'I told her I was having a kick-about with Conor,' said Theo, looking slightly guilty. 'I wanted to have some Strike Club time. I'll be OK to get back at 4.30 too.'

'Go on then!' said Lizzie. 'No time to waste, sitting around talking! Go! We'll see you at the school at 6.30. After we've sucked up some energy.'

'Wait,' said Theo. 'Let me just write down what that FLT said.'

'What's an FLT?' asked Doug.

'A Faceless Loomy Thing,' said both Theo and Alisha at the same time. Doug and Lizzie hooted with laughter (although Doug's laugh was very low volume).

Doug repeated the Chaucerian quote—shouting out the spelling as his energy faded further—and Theo scribbled it down on a scrap of paper from his school bag.

Then Lizzie and Doug went off to sneakily lower the body temperature of most of the kids in the playground. 'Gives a new meaning to the phrase "chilling out", doesn't it?' said Alisha as she and Doug headed back towards the road. The FLTs had now gone completely and it was a relief to feel the sun on their skin and not have its warmth immediately evaporate. 'How long to walk to the *Echo* office?' asked Alisha.

'Um—about fifteen minutes,' said Theo.

Alisha hitched up her school bag. 'Seven if we run.'

There was no report of any fire in the whole of Beechwood Junior School's history. Jez, the librarian who had helped Theo out before, gave them a pale-brown paper folder filled with yellowed paper cuttings.

'Sorry,' he said. 'We're getting all this stuff scanned in and available online but it takes forever. We haven't even got past the 1920s yet!'

It was quite easy for them to look through the cuttings. There was a report from 1927 when the school was officially opened by Easthampton's mayor and then a sheaf of other stories—sporting triumphs, new headmaster appointments, school plays, and even, in recent years, Ofsted reports. If there ever had been a fire at the school, nobody had reported it to the *Echo*.

'And anyway,' said Alisha. 'The ghosts I saw looked *older* than that. Their clothes weren't twentieth century clothes.'

'So maybe it was a fire on the *site* of the school—from way before it was built,' suggested Theo. He suddenly clicked his tongue in frustration. 'I didn't tell Doug and Lizzie about what was on the stone! The writing. That might have helped.' He opened his bag and pulled out his notebook. On the page before Doug's Chaucer quote he'd copied down the Latin from the broken stone, along with Mr Carter's partial translation.

'Maybe that's Middle English too,' said Alisha.

'No, it's Latin,' said Theo. 'Mr Carter said so—but I think they used Latin a lot back then. It was all sort of mixed in with the English. The priests and the high-born people used to use it most. I think they called it "High Speech".'

Alisha sat up and regarded him for a few seconds, her head on one side. 'Theo—how come you remember all this stuff? When we first met, you told me you could never keep anything in your head.'

Theo shrugged and grinned at her across the pile of cuttings. 'What . . . back when I was a lame brain?'

She felt herself blush at her own unkind words.

'Well, that's what 70,000 volts does for you, I guess,' he said. 'If it doesn't kill you first.'

Alisha took his notebook and peered at the words from the old ghost.

CHAUCER: Privee theef men clepeth Deeth.

'Is that spelt right?' she asked.

'That's how Doug spelt it out,' said Theo. 'Middle English spelling!'

'Hmmm,' said Alisha, deep in thought. Then she got up and went over to Jez. 'Um . . . would we be able to look something up on the internet while we're here?' she asked.

'Sure,' he said, waving her over to a laptop on a desk at the other end of the small library. 'You won't need a password. Go for it. I've got to deliver some stuff to the editor—I'll be back in a few minutes.'

'Thanks,' said Alisha and headed straight for the laptop. Theo followed her and leaned on the back of her chair as she pulled up the search engine page and carefully typed in the old Middle English sentence. It was so odd, she really didn't expect to get much back. So she let out a 'Woohoo!' of surprise when a torrent of hits arrived. The first was from a site called ASK ME! and the top line of the response read: **What is pestilence?**

Alisha glanced at Theo. He was frowning as if trying to remember something. She clicked on the page and immediately more words were flung up:

The fourteenth century English poet Geoffrey Chaucer spoke of 'pestilence' in 'The Pardoner's Tale':

Ther cam a privee theef men clepeth Deeth,
That in this contree al the peple sleeth,
And with his spere he smoot his herte atwo,
And wente his wey withouten wordes mo.
He hath a thousand slayn this pestilence.

Pestilence is also one of the Four Horsemen of the Apocalypse, along with War, Famine, and Death. It refers to the <u>Black Death</u>.

Alisha turned, wordlessly, to Theo. He was staring at the short article on the screen, something dawning on his face. Suddenly he scrabbled for the notebook and flipped the page over to the incomplete Latin inscription:

unqua . . . cio . . . pro . . . ligeo . . . STILENC

He showed it to Alisha, pointing at the last incomplete word—the one that had arrived, graven in stone, on his desk that morning.

. . . stilenc . . .

Then he pointed to the screen and the final word of the Chaucerian poem.

Pestilence.

'Stilenc . . . pestilence,' she murmured. 'Black Death.' She drew in a long breath and then suddenly her fingers were dancing across the keyboard again. She typed 'images of the Black Death' into the search box and in seconds a gallery of grim pictures lay before them. Some were old etchings of people on their deathbeds or being laid to rest, obviously dating back centuries, but others were actual photographs of more recent victims—and these were what made Alisha give a frightened whimper of recognition. Pale bodies with blacked noses, chins, and ears, swollen eyes; lumpen black growths in armpits.

'This is them!' she whispered. 'These look exactly like the ghosts haunting me today. Theo . . . none of them died in a fire! They all died of the plague!'

CHAPTER TWENTY-TWO

'I'm worried,' said Doug. Below him a family of four trudged home, looking tired and slightly baffled. They'd all arrived at the park with such energy, ready to play rounders, and then abruptly got very tired and chilly. Only some chocolate from the ice-cream van had perked them up enough for the walk home. 'I think we might all be coming down with something,' said the mother, with a shiver.

'So you *should* be worried,' said Lizzie, catching up with him. 'Leave the poor things alone now! You've nicked far too much energy off them!'

'Oh—oops. Sorry,' said Doug, detaching his spiritual presence from the drooping family with an apologetic wave. They perked up seconds later.

'No—I'm worried about Alisha and Theo,' went on Doug. 'Why were those old spirits following them around? Why are they looming about at their school? I just couldn't get enough from them; they were too exhausted from travelling so far to really tell me anything helpful.'

'I'm worried too,' admitted Lizzie. 'Spirits don't warn people lightly, especially spirits *that* old. I keep thinking about the way they were—what was it Alisha said—blackened? Like they'd been caught up in a fire . . . Dougie, what if there's going to be a fire?'

'But why bother showing me that bit of Chaucer's poem?' said Doug. 'How does *that* connect with fire? The Great Fire of London, maybe?'

'No—that was 1666,' said Lizzie. 'Chaucer was a fourteenth-century guy. Whatever it is, we've got to keep powering up and get down to that school for half past six,' said Lizzie. 'Come on—there's a bunch of teenagers sitting by the lake. They'll do nicely.'

'Teenagers?' scoffed Doug. 'After school? They'll be horizontal!'

'Nope. They're playing multi-player games on laptops,' said Lizzie. 'They'll be supercharged, sweaty, happy bunnies. Let's go and do the ghosty vampire thing!'

'OK,' said Doug. 'We can have the WiFi for dessert.'

CHAPTER TWENTY-THREE

Alisha realized her mistake as soon as Kirsty opened the door in her disco-vampire outfit.

'Oh! Alisha!' she squeaked, with a wide fake smile. She glanced quickly back over her shoulder. 'We didn't think you were coming!'

'Why wouldn't I?' asked Alisha, trying to smile and sound normal when her insides were churning and her hands were shaking because a) her new friends were probably just about to reject her and b) she was in fear of the Black Death.

'Well . . . when you went off with Theo instead of sitting with us at lunchtime, we thought . . . you know,' Kirsty smirked. 'That you'd found better things to do than hang out with us.'

'No,' protested Alisha. 'Look—we just had to do some research.'

Sophie came down the stairs behind Kirsty and at the top, peering over the banister, were Emma and Rosie. They were all in their outfits already and clearly the hair and make up session had started. 'What kind of research?' giggled Kirsty. 'Like . . . snogging research?' All the girls exploded into fits of laughter.

'NO!' said Alisha, hotly. 'Nothing like *that*. Actually . . . really *important* research. About the school's history. About—look—I just came to warn you.'

The laughter subsided and Sophie bit her lip while Kirsty took a deep breath and said: 'Warn us . . . about what?'

Now that she'd said the words, Alisha found herself opening and closing her mouth like a goldfish. She didn't know how to put it.

'Well?' asked Kirsty, and her voice had lost all its fake chumminess. 'What? That you're going to be weird again all evening? That you'll be sneaking off to play kiss chase with Theo? That you'll disco dance like a dead girl?' More giggling came from behind her.

Alisha took a deep breath. 'Are you all feeling OK?' she asked, as calmly as she could.

There was a moment of baffled silence. Kirsty blinked. 'Are we feeling OK? Yes! We're feeling *fine*. How about you? You don't look too good. You look pretty awful, in fact—and you haven't even put the white makeup on yet!'

'I mean . . . do any of you feel a bit . . . fluey,' went on Alisha, lamely. 'And . . . do your armpits hurt?'

Kirsty rolled her eyes. 'Look, Alisha—we don't want to be unkind but you are so freaking us out. Maybe you'd better just go home, eh? Or maybe Theo will take you to the disco,' she added, with a snort.

'He will,' said Alisha, with a sigh. 'He's waiting at the gate. I wasn't planning to come in. I have more important things to do now. See you later . . . although, you might want to think about not coming back to the school tonight.'

'Why?' Kirsty demanded, looking suddenly quite rattled.

'For your health,' said Alisha, and walked away.

On the far side of a tall hedge, Theo waited. 'Well?'

'They seem OK,' said Alisha. 'They look healthy enough. But we've got to get to the school and check the building site before we can be sure.'

Theo was wearing a new shirt and jeans and his mother had made an attempt to calm down his spiky hair, but it was already sticking up on end again. He'd picked up Alisha, in her white dress, at her place just after six and both had promised to walk straight to the school. They would be collected at half past nine along with all the other kids. If they made it to half past nine.

'You asked about the armpits?'

'Yes,' said Alisha. 'That went down a treat. As if I could get any weirder.'

'Well—at least you checked,' he said. 'If they felt anything like mine did today, they'd know about it. You'd have seen a reaction.'

'And fever and sickness,' said Alisha. 'That must have been horrible.'

'It was,' said Theo. 'And it was only a ghost version of it. I'm sure the FLTs were making me feel that way to get the message across.'

'Do you—do you really think there's plague at the school?' said Alisha. 'How can that *be*? That stuff all died out centuries ago.'

'You'd think,' said Theo. 'But the last bad outbreak in the UK was in the 1900s . . . Mr Carter was telling us about it just today. And it's still being reported in countries around the world. Someone in China died from it a few years back.'

'But how could it possibly be at our school?' said Alisha.

'I don't know . . . but Lizzie said hauntings often happen when there's disruption. And there's been digging. I think it's to do with that,' said Theo.

CHAPTER TWENTY-THREE

'Maybe it's still in the soil, somehow.'

When they arrived at the school only a few kids and teachers were there, ambling in and out of the double doors which opened from the school hall directly onto the playground. Inside the hall music stopped and started and one of the teachers made popping noises into a microphone. They were still getting ready.

Theo and Alisha skirted the far side of the playground as they passed the hall and went around to the building site at the back. It was deserted and fenced with bright orange mesh on low metal posts. This was easy to step over, though, and they both slipped across it, glancing back to be sure they weren't seen. Theo followed the line of trenches that he'd first seen a few days ago when Chris the builder had been digging in them. The footings were now filled with solid grey cement.

'See anything?' Theo asked.

Alisha shook her head. 'Nothing. Maybe we're wrong. Or maybe the cement has settled everything down again. You seeing any Faceless Loomy Things?'

'No. Maybe they've used up all their energy for now and can't loom for a bit,' said Theo. He walked further on to the building site and then stopped at a deep pit in the soil. There was no concrete in it—

just more brown earth and grey rubble. 'What's this for?'

Alisha shrugged. 'I don't know . . . maybe for plumbing or something. Or perhaps they're digging a cellar.' She leaned carefully over, looking into the dim pit, which was deeper than they were tall.

She felt the chill at exactly the moment Theo gasped. 'Can you see it?' he whispered, dropping to his hands and knees and staring down into the pit. And she could. A tiny smoky twist of grey, spiralling up towards them.

'Can you see *those*?' she murmured.

'The green things?'

'Yes.'

For there were tiny green specks in the smoke. Tiny green specks which seemed to spin and writhe in the darkness like living things.

'Old ghosts have no colour left,' breathed Alisha. 'They're too dead. Too long gone. So what are *they*?'

'They're not ghosts,' gulped Theo, suddenly pulling her back from the drop. 'They're *living*.' He looked at her, his face grim. 'Like a virus. We're right. We've got to stop this. We've got to warn everyone.'

They ran back to the orange mesh fencing and

leapt across it like athletes. By the time they reached the hall they could see it had filled up over the past few minutes. Most of the kids in school were there now, and a good half of them were already dancing in the multicoloured disco lights.

'Who are we going to tell?' panted Alisha, doing her best not to look across to Kirsty and the girls, who were bopping in the centre of the floor, looking cool and confident.

'Mr Carter!' said Theo. 'He knows about history and he translated the Latin on those bits of the stone. And we know what it is now, don't we? We can tell him and he'll believe us!'

Mr Carter was helping with the disco music, flicking though some old vinyl discs, nodding his head in time to the track that was playing. Alisha and Theo almost skidded into him.

'Whoa! Steady!' called the teacher. 'What's up with you two?'

'Sir,' said Theo, his voice shrill above the music. 'We really need to talk to you.'

'OK—well, fire away!' yelled Mr Carter, re-stacking the pile of vinyl.

'No—please. We need to talk PROPERLY!' insisted Alisha, and at last the man noticed their expressions. He led the way into the corridor, letting the heavy doors fall shut behind them to block out most of the music.

'What is it?' he asked, looking perplexed and flushed in his bright disco shirt.

'We have to get everyone out of the school,' said Alisha. 'It's an emergency!'

Mr Carter frowned. 'An emergency? What—is there a fire?'

'No! No it's worse than that!' said Theo. 'There's plague!'

Mr Carter paused with his mouth open for a few moments and then seemed to notice the white ghostly dress Alisha was in. 'Ooh, I get it! Very funny,' he said, chuckling. 'I heard there was a big Friday the thirteenth thing going on.'

Theo actually grabbed his arm. 'NO! No—this isn't a joke. Seriously, sir—there's plague in the school. The Black Death! Alisha and me . . . we've seen it.'

The grin slid from the teacher's face. As an Abba hit boomed away behind the door, he said, 'Look— both of you. I want you to come to the head's office with me. I'm going to call your parents.'

'What? Why?!' spluttered Theo. 'We don't need them to come here! We just need to get everyone out and call ambulances and get them checked over.'

'Theo—listen to yourself. You're hysterical,' said Mr Carter. 'And I don't blame you—this whole lightning strike business would mess anyone up. It's not your fault but I really think you should be taken home. Both of you.'

'BUT THE STONE!' bawled Theo. 'The Latin on the STONE! We know what it means! It's a warning. We looked it up: *stilenc* is part of PESTILENCIE!'

'Wait here,' said Mr Carter and then he opened the school hall doors and began yelling for back-up.

'Come on!' yelled Alisha, grabbing Theo's arm. 'Back to your classroom—we have to show him.'

And they ran, knowing the teacher would be forced to follow. Mr Carter gave a shout and then hurtled after them before he'd managed to get any attention across the loud thudding of 'Dancing Queen'.

They pounded into the classroom twenty seconds later, the door smashing hard against the wall. Theo was unwrapping the bits of stone as Mr Carter arrived.

'Listen you two—you have to sit down and listen to me!' he was pleading. He was panicky and sweaty and he suddenly slumped onto a chair, looking exhausted.

'No,' said Alisha. 'You have to listen to *us*.' She sounded calmer than before—and that was probably because 'us' was not just the two of them anymore. Lizzie and Doug had just materialized on either side of Theo.

'You're both right,' said Doug. 'It's plague. We can see it now. You have to get everybody out.'

'I'm going to tell him,' said Alisha. 'All of it.'

'Go on then,' said Mr Carter, still puffing from the run and looking even sweatier. 'Whatever you need to tell me, please. I'm all ears.' He pointed to his ears and then winced.

'Wait,' said Theo. 'Mr Carter . . . do your armpits hurt?'

The teacher stared at Theo in astonishment and then murmured, 'Yes. Yes, they do. They've been hurting for a couple of hours. I thought I'd overdone it, hanging the disco decorations up . . .'

'Chris's armpits were hurting him yesterday,' said Theo. 'Alisha saw him being sick on the way home from school. And his mate tried to pull him up and he was in pain under his arms.'

Mr Carter absorbed what they were saying for a few seconds, a dawning realization in his eyes.

'Show him the stones,' said Lizzie.

'I will, but there are still letters missing,' said Theo.

'Who are you talking to, Theo?' said Mr Carter, glancing around.

'Look at these,' said Theo, and he and Alisha held out the broken stones, close together so he could see the inscription, or what there was of it:

unqua . . . cio . . . pro . . . ligeo . . . STILENC

'Me and Alisha went to the cuttings library at the *Echo* and did some research. This Latin . . . we think we know what it means . . . it's—um . . .'

'*Nunquam patefacio pro religio pestilencie*,' said Douglas into Theo's ear.

'*Nunquam patefacio pro religio pestilencie*,' repeated Theo. 'And translated, that means . . .'

'Oh dear God,' murmured Mr Carter.

'Never open for fear of pestilence,' said Theo.

'Oh dear God,' said the teacher, again. 'It's a plague pit. The builders. They've struck a plague pit.'

And then he collapsed on to the floor.

CHAPTER TWENTY-FOUR

Alisha used one of the stones to smash the glass on the fire alarm. On the floor Mr Carter groaned, his eyes closed.

'He's really hot,' said Theo, touching the man's forehead. 'This is for real! He's burning up!'

Doug and Lizzie knelt down too and Lizzie put her hand through Mr Carter's chest.

'Is his heart all right?' asked Alisha, feeling her insides quaking. Suddenly everything was so much worse. As terrifying as the ghosts and the green flecks and the swirling grey presence had been, a living person suddenly so ill was scarier still.

'I don't know,' said Lizzie. 'I'm just trying to cool him down.'

'We need to get to a phone—call an ambulance,' yelled Theo above the raucous din of the fire alarm. 'They'll be sending fire crews, I guess—but maybe not ambulances. Alisha—you have to get to reception and dial 999.'

Alisha ran down the corridor. As she grabbed the phone in reception she could see everyone piling out into the playground. The teachers and parents were looking concerned but not panicked. They probably thought this was just a prank. She must call an ambulance now.

'Emergency services—which service do you require?' said a woman on the line.

'My name is Alisha and I'm a pupil at Beechwood Junior School,' she said, trying to sound serious and grown up. 'There's an emergency. We need lots of ambulances. I'm NOT joking. PLEASE—send ambulances.'

'What is the nature of the emerg—' Alisha put the phone down. She knew any more information would not help. Now she must get a teacher to come and see to Mr Carter.

But as she ran outside she realized something terrible was happening. The children and teachers had filed out sensibly into the playground . . . but, exactly as the school emergency evacuation plan instructed, they had not stopped there. They had moved on to the 'safer' muster point on the edge of the school field.

They were all gathering *right next to* the building site and the deep pit. And now, rising up into the air just metres away, swirling around and around in eddies of air created by the movement of the crowd, was a grim cloud of bubbling grey. And in the cloud were thousands—no—*millions* of writhing green specks.

Alisha ran, screaming, towards them. 'GO BACK!' she shrieked, waving them back towards the playground. 'GO BACK! AWAY FROM THE BUILDING SITE! THE PLAGUE IS COMING OUT! IT'LL GET YOU!'

And it would. In fact, for some, it already had. She could see Kirsty and Sophie, right next to the orange mesh fence, laughing at her and inhaling a stream of green specks as they did so. They were dragging Black Death right down into their lungs and they had no idea.

Nobody moved of course. Except a couple of teachers who came running, ready to grab her and calm her down. But Alisha turned on her heel and sped back across the playground, slamming through the empty hall, where the disco lights still played forlornly on the walls and ceiling but Abba had been silenced.

She found Theo, Lizzie, and Doug still crouched over Mr Carter, who was groaning and trying to sit up. 'They're rising up from the building site! Plague specks! Everyone's standing right next to them and I can't make them move!' she yelled. 'Lizzie! Doug! You've got to help me! We have to make them move!!!'

Lizzie and Doug looked at each other. 'Can we?' said Lizzie.

'We've got enough juice to get out there,' said Doug. 'And we can get some more from everyone outside.'

'No—the older ghosts will need all the juice from the crowd. We haven't a hope of raising them otherwise.' Lizzie glanced at Alisha and Theo. 'We'll have to attach. We'll have to walk IN them.'

Doug turned to look at their living, breathing friends. 'It won't be nice. Theo might pass out again. They might both pass out.'

'No I won't,' said Theo. 'Whatever you're both talking about—just do it!'

'Come on,' said Lizzie. 'You'll have to leave your teacher here for a few minutes. We need to get outside, get organized, and get help.'

Mrs Gardner was running down the corridor, looking for Alisha. Then she was spun aside as the girl suddenly ran back past her with Theo thundering alongside her. 'Mr Carter's sick!' yelled Theo, as he passed. 'In class! Help him!' She ran a few metres further and glanced into her colleague's classroom. They heard her shout of concern as she saw him on the floor. There was no time to help her.

'OK,' said Doug. 'You'll have to stay in step with us and we'll use up a lot of your energy. It won't be nice.'

'Do it,' said Theo.

He and Alisha shivered as they walked towards the orange mesh fence. They were so cold their teeth were chattering. Theo could see the grey cloud, filled with writhing green specks, like tiny maggots, rising high into the air. It was beginning to topple over and tumble like a slow waterfall, towards the crowd beneath. It had already reached maybe half a dozen of the kids closest to it.

Doug walked in step with Theo—merging his spirit shape with Theo's living shape. Lizzie did the same with Alisha. 'Don't pass out on me now,' Doug said, as Theo's head swam. 'Stay with me. I need your energy.'

Then there was a freezing cold whoosh running right through Theo's chest and up through his head, as if he was in a vertical wind tunnel. He could hardly see through it but he could hear Doug shouting: 'Now! We need you NOW! SHOW YOURSELVES!' As

CHAPTER TWENTY-FOUR

Theo's vision cleared, he realized the FLTs were back.

'LOOK!' yelled Alisha, next to him. She pointed up and the cloud of grey seemed to thicken with shapes, moving and swaying. Some of them walked out of the base of the cloud; the small, pale, blackened ones she had seen earlier that day.

'We all need more juice!' yelled Lizzie. 'Or the living will never see them!'

Alisha felt light-headed and chilled to the bone. Still walking with Lizzie sharing her space, she arrived close to the girls who were almost certainly not her friends any more. Alisha grabbed Theo's arm and then her other hand shot out and she snagged Kirsty's wrist. 'Hey, vampire girl,' she said, grinning. 'We need your life force!'

'Get OFF me, you freak!' retorted Kirsty, trying to break free. But Alisha would not let go and of course, the others soon started trying to drag their friend away, connecting life force to life force and sending a big fat pulse of panicky energy through to Lizzie and Doug and linking them with the crowd.

The FLTs got more substantial as Lizzie and Doug passed the energy along. With the flashing disco lights feeding through from the hall windows and shafting through them, they had never looked more eerie.

At last the screaming started.

Very soon the crowd was running for the playground. Not everyone saw the dead people but five or six more sensitive ones did. Two of these were well-respected teachers and the sight of *them* backing away in horror was enough to get the whole school off the playing field and back to the concrete.

By the time they reached the school gates a fleet of ambulances and fire engines was swinging through them. No children at all were left in the downdraft of the plague.

Except two.

Doug and Lizzie had been wiped out along with the flaky, shaky FLTs the second they lost contact with the crowd.

And Theo and Alisha—two human fireworks all the while they had channelled everyone's energy through to the spirit world—sparked, sputtered, fell to the ground.

And lay still.

CHAPTER TWENTY-FIVE

They were kept on a drip for three days. They didn't wake up for the first day and when they regained consciousness on day two, they discovered their beds were side by side on the children's ward.

'The doctors think you were both too weak to have gone back to school,' said Mum, smoothing Alisha's hair. 'I *knew* it—and so did Theo's mum. And then, with all the excitement and the plague scare . . .'

Alisha stared up from her pillow. 'So . . . we were right. There *was* plague at the school.'

'Yes, sweetheart,' said Mum, looking quite appalled. 'I can't believe it! How on earth did you and Theo find out?'

'It was the chunks of stone that Theo . . . found,' explained Alisha. 'They had Latin lettering on them and we looked it up and it said something like *Don't open this unless you want to catch plague.* It was Theo who worked it out. He's really good at history.'

Theo, sitting up in the next bed along, beamed.

'Yeah,' he said. 'But only since I got struck by lightning. And anyway—if Alisha hadn't remembered seeing Chris being sick and having sore armpits, we'd never have worked out the plague was back.'

'Sore armpits?' said Alisha's mum, raising an eyebrow.

'Buboes!' said Theo, grinning. 'Swellings in the armpits and neck and groin . . . they go all black and then they bur—'

'What's happened to everyone?' cut in Alisha, watching her mother turn a little pale. 'Mr Carter? And Chris, the builder? They got sick. Are they . . . are they dead?'

'No,' said her mum. 'Chris is in intensive care. Mr Carter told the paramedics they had to find him and all the other builders. A couple of the other guys caught it too. Chris was really bad when the paramedics got to his flat. He had those . . . bubo things you're talking about, Theo. In fact, the whole school and all the surrounding neighbourhood is being treated with antibiotics. Mr Carter was pretty bad, too—but he's getting better.' She shuddered. 'I still can't believe it! Plague! Right here in the twenty-first century . . . in our town! There are men in masks and white suits all over the school grounds. And telly cameras and reporters everywhere too!'

'Have they found out where it's coming from?' asked Theo.

'Apparently there's a plague pit right underneath the school field,' said Alisha's mum. 'Just a small one—about thirty or so people. They were all buried together and then stones were laid over the pit with warnings engraved on them. Just like the bits of stone you found. But that all got covered up over time. It's really rare for this to happen, but the bacteria somehow survived through centuries, deep in the soil under the stones. If the builders hadn't dug up that bit of the school field, we'd never have known.'

'Have *we* got it?' asked Alisha, staring at the plastic line running into her wrist.

'No, sweetheart. You two are fine! You've been given antibiotics anyway, as a precaution. You'll have to stay here another day or so and then you can come home and get your strength back up.'

It was all over the news of course—and not just the local or even the UK news. The story went worldwide within hours. Happily, for Alisha, she wasn't at the centre of it this time. Mr Carter, recovering well from his brush with the Black Death, told the press about the chunks of stone and a gifted historian in his class who'd helped him to work out what was going on.

'Theo did some research on the Latin inscription.

He recognized the word "pestilence" and then, when I got sick, he recognized the symptoms,' Mr Carter told the reporters, from his hospital bed. 'We'd just been doing the plague in history.' Theo and Alisha and a couple of intrigued nurses watched the interview on the little telly in the children's ward on day three of their stay. The press had filmed Theo too, but not Alisha—she had been quite firm that she wanted to stay out of it this time.

As if the plague story wasn't sensational enough, there was a lot of talk about people seeing 'a cloud of death' on the school field on the evening of the disco—but the head teacher had put that down to a bonfire nearby and lots of overexcited children dressed up in spooky outfits, their imaginations running away with them.

'Did you two see this big black cloud?' Theo's mum asked, later that week, as they were being signed out of the hospital.

'We were so freaked out, trying to let everyone know, *all* we could see were people killed by plague,' said Alisha . . . mostly truthfully. 'We nearly *all* ended up as ghosts.'

'I can't take much more of this,' muttered Mum.

'You saved lives, you know,' said Theo's mum, Jenna. 'Some of the kids were going away on holiday on the weekend. They would have been on planes and boats and trains and if they'd caught the disease and gone off without treatment . . .' She shivered. 'It could have been too late for them. Not every country has access to the right antibiotics. And they could have spread the plague all over the world! It *is* treatable,' she added. 'But only if you catch it early enough.'

The whole school and its grounds were sealed off. They would be fumigated and the bacteria killed across the summer holidays. A team of archaeologists would excavate the burial pit as soon as it was considered safe by the white-suited men in masks. There would be a bit of a delay on the building of the new library.

'What a summer it's been!' murmured Alisha's mum, as they drove home. 'Lightning strikes, plague . . . what next? A swarm of locusts?'

CHAPTER TWENTY-SIX

The common was very quiet. Hardly anyone was there, even though it was a lovely late-July day with a clear blue sky and the lightest of summer breezes. The plague scare had done nothing for tourism in Easthampton, and many of the local kids were being kept in until their parents were completely sure there was no risk.

Theo and Alisha lay on the grass by the ornamental lake, just a short distance from the dead lightning tree, listening to grasshoppers chirruping in the long grass and watching the occasional pigeon flit overhead. They were very quiet too. Theo tapped idly on the cardboard box in the grass next to him.

'*How* much did you pay?' asked Alisha, at length.

'Nearly two hundred,' said Theo.

Alisha gave a low whistle. 'I'll put half in,' she said.

'You don't have to,' said Theo. 'I used my award money. Most of it. Mam thinks I got it for you. She thinks it's really sweet.'

'As if,' said Alisha. 'But I'm giving you half anyway. I want to.' They had both been invited to Easthampton's mayoral chambers earlier that week and presented with a small medal and £250 each. More photos in the paper. Apparently they were community heroes. Theo was loving it and Alisha . . . well, she was *managing* it.

'OK,' said Theo. 'But it might all be for nothing if they NEVER SHOW UP AGAIN!' His rising shout met only with a brief lull before the grasshopper chirruping resumed.

'This is the third day in a row,' said Alisha. 'What if . . . what if they don't come back?'

Theo sighed. 'Or what if they're here but we just can't see them anymore?'

Alisha didn't answer. That was a horrible thought. It had taken a week to be allowed out of the house—and that was after three days in hospital. It was now nearly two weeks since the plague night at school and they hadn't seen Doug and Lizzie once. They hadn't even caught a shadow, or a drift of mist, or so much as a cool chill on the back of the neck. They'd been to Doug's gravestone and all around the cemetery until they'd found Lizzie's too. Nothing. Nothing by the lightning tree or the oak tree where she and Theo had been struck, or here by the lake—one of Lizzie and Doug's favourite haunts. They'd come back every day for the last three days. Nothing.

'Where do you think they've gone?' she asked Theo. 'Do you think they've . . . you know . . . moved on?'

'What—to heaven or something?'

Alisha shrugged and picked the petals off a daisy. 'Lizzie said they didn't want to go yet. They liked it fine just here—especially after we made Strike Club. Why would they leave us without saying goodbye?'

'They're our friends,' said Theo. 'They *would* have said goodbye.'

'But what if . . . ?'

'Well, you'll be stuck with just me, won't you?' snapped Theo. 'Unless you want to get back in with Kirsty and her lot.'

Alisha considered this. 'She does want to be friends,' she said, yawning and stretching on the grass. 'But probably only because we saved her life. She was meant to be flying out to Greece with her family two days after the disco. By the time they'd diagnosed her it might well have been too late and she knows that. The others have been really nice to me, too. Sophie phoned up said sorry about how mean they were to me before the disco.'

'You see—it's easy to make friends,' snorted Theo. 'You just save them from the Black Death.'

'Well . . . I'm not sure I really care any more,' said Alisha. 'I mean, it'll be nice if they stay friendly; nice to be included. But . . . I'd rather hang out with Strike Club. Even if that's only *you* now.' She sighed. 'I really hope it's not, though.'

A little way down by the water's edge, some ducklings and their mother duck suddenly scattered across the lake, looking alarmed.

'Can't we try now?' asked Lizzie, blowing some duck feathers after them. 'Surely they're up to it today?'

'OK—but only quickly,' said Doug. 'They're still too weak. And so are we.'

'Come on then!' urged Lizzie. 'I have to know what's in that box!'

'They're HERE!' yelled Alisha, delightedly springing up on to her knees as their two friends wafted into view nearby.

'Can't stay long!' said Doug, fading in and out. 'We're still wiped out. And you're too feeble to fuel us up! Another twenty-four hours should do it. There's a football match down on the lower common tomorrow. Twenty-two fit kids to mess with. We're going to juice up.'

'OK! We'll come back tomorrow!' said Alisha.

'We'll eat a massive lunch!' promised Theo, on his feet, clutching the box.

'What's in the box?' asked Lizzie as she started to fade.

'I'll show you tomorrow,' said Theo. 'You'd better come back! And strong too! Because we need to take you somewhere.'

Their friends were glancing at each other and looking intrigued as they dissolved from view.

'Are you sure?' asked Alisha. 'Are you sure it's a good idea?'

'Yes,' said Theo. 'Because even ghosts can be haunted.'

CHAPTER TWENTY-SEVEN

She lived in a neat, terraced cottage with a wrought iron front gate and a herringbone brick path that led past clumps of fragrant heather to the front door.

'We'll wait at the gate,' said Lizzie. Alisha nodded. This was Theo's plan and she didn't want to crash it.

'OK,' said Theo. 'You alright, Dougie? You look a bit pale . . .'

'Oh ha ha!' said Doug, but he *was* pale. Anxious too. 'Are you sure you want to do this?' he said as they reached the front door, which was painted green and had stained glass at the top.

'Yes,' said Theo. 'You helped *us*—hundreds of us. And now I want to help you.'

'She might freak out,' said Doug.

'I don't think so,' said Theo and knocked.

Karen Rathbone smiled as soon as she opened the door and saw him. 'That's funny,' she said, over the barking of her terrier. 'I was just thinking about you—and about Dougie. How strange!'

'I-I wanted to talk to you,' said Theo, feeling a little hot and self-conscious now that the moment had arrived. He'd been planning what he would say for a week.

'Wait,' Karen said, glancing back. 'I'll put Barney in the kitchen and get us lemonade. Have a seat.' She pointed to a sun-warmed wooden bench beneath the front room window. Theo sat in the middle and Dougie sat to his right. He was a cool, steady presence. He wasn't flickering. He and Lizzie had spent hours siphoning energy at the common today. Alisha and Lizzie had edged away behind a neighbour's hedge but both were peeping out and giving a thumbs-up.

Karen came out carrying two tall glasses filled with cloudy lemonade and chinking ice cubes. 'I can't believe what I've been reading about you,' she said, sitting down to Theo's left and passing him a glass. 'All the plague pit stuff right after the lightning strike business. You couldn't make it up! They came round and tested me too, you know! But it seems I'm plague free.' She smiled again, sipped some lemonade, and glanced at the box on his knee. 'So . . . what's all this about, Theo?'

'Um . . .' How to start? 'It's kind of . . . about Dougie,' he said, also taking a gulp of lemonade and then putting the glass on the bench beside him, right through Doug's knee.

And then Karen made it easy. She smiled again and nodded. 'I thought so. You know, Theo—you'll probably think I'm mad, but I often think he's here with me. I feel his presence.'

'Can you feel it now?' asked Theo.

'Oh yes, very definitely. Right here in the garden. Probably sitting right next to you.' She gave a little laugh and rested her drink down by her feet.

'You're right,' said Theo. 'He is.'

She nodded again. She probably thought *he* was humouring *her*.

'I've met Dougie,' he said. 'I've talked to him.'

She tilted her head to one side and pushed her glasses a little higher on her nose. 'Really . . . ? In . . . in dreams, maybe?'

'Well, it was at night,' said Theo. 'That's when he told me about you.'

'Oh, I see.' She paused. Waiting. She didn't seem like she would freak out whatever he said, and he hoped he was right.

'The thing is, he knows how bad you feel about the last thing you said to him,' said Theo. 'And— believe it or not—*he* feels really bad too.'

Her face didn't move but she gulped and her eyes

began to well up. 'What do you think I said to him, Theo?' she asked, softly.

'You were just a kid,' said Theo. 'And you had no idea that he actually *would.*'

She caught her breath, then, and gripped the edge of the seat.

Drop dead! She had shouted *Drop dead!*

Theo knew he was crossing the line. He pushed on anyway. 'He was messing with your stuff and he picked up your most favourite thing and dunked it in the pond,' he said. 'Anyone would have been angry.'

'How . . . how could you *know* that?' she whispered. 'Nobody knows that! I never even told Mum and Dad.'

'So . . . he wants you to stop feeling bad. To stop blaming yourself,' said Theo. 'He says he's sorry. And he wants you to have this.'

She took the box and eased off the lid with trembling hands. Inside it was another box. It was pink-and-white striped with a cellophane panel. Beyond the cellophane a Sindy Active Ballerina was doing the splits. She had dark glossy hair pulled into a bun and wore white mesh tights, a white leotard, and a lilac tutu skirt. *15 MOVEABLE JOINTS* promised a label above the Pedigree logo. The doll inside had been wired into her graceful pose for decades. She'd never been out of her box, which was what had made her such a collector's item and so expensive when Theo had found her on the internet.

Karen began to laugh and cry at the same time. She swiftly broke the seals and lifted the lid, undid the little ties binding the doll to the packaging, and pulled her free. The Sindy instantly lost about £160 in value. Karen put her into a dancer's pose, arms up and arched above her head, one ballet-shoed foot on her palm and the other raised out behind her. Karen lifted her high, chuckling with delight.

'Oh my!' she murmured, tears tracking down her face. 'Thank you! Thank you, Dougie!'

'He says you're welcome,' said Theo.

She gave him a tight, tearful hug and as coolness cascaded over his skin, Theo knew it was mostly Dougie hugging her back.

CHAPTER TWENTY-EIGHT

'Wind chimes,' said Theo, as he and Alisha wandered home. 'Brilliant idea. Dougie told me to tell her to put wind chimes in a corner of the house which gets no breeze. And now every time he looks in on her and wants her to know, he can make them chime.'

'That's so lovely,' said Alisha. 'Wow! She believed you. She didn't think you were mad. And she *loved* that doll. You made her so happy.'

Theo looked a little pink as they ambled on. Lizzie and Doug had vanished soon after the part-real, part-spirit hug for Karen. All the emotion was exhausting and they just couldn't hang on so far from the common.

'That was a very special thing you did,' said Alisha, handing him ten ten-pound notes. 'I'm glad I could pay for half of it, but I might never have been brave enough to go and talk to her. What if she'd decided you were bonkers?!'

Theo shrugged. And then blinked in surprise as

Alisha suddenly gave him a little awkward hug and planted a warm kiss on his cheek.

'Whoa—steady on!' he squawked. 'Look!' He pointed along the road to where Kirsty Fellows and Sophie Clarke were sitting on a garden wall and gawping at them.

Alisha gave them a little wave. 'I don't care,' she laughed. 'I'm proud of you, Theodore. You know . . . one day . . .'

'Don't go there, Alisha!' he warned, giving her a shove.

'No, *really*,' she giggled, shoving him back. 'One day you might even make president . . .'

ACKNOWLEDGEMENTS

This book was written in public libraries around Hampshire, England. My great thanks to the kind staff of the following sanctuaries:

Gosport Discovery Centre
Eastleigh Library
Petersfield Library
Fleet Library
Southampton Central Library

Don't know where I'd be without you.

Thanks also to the Southampton Daily Echo library for allowing me to fossick about in its old cuttings and Dr Anna Blackwell for very useful medical guidance.

And to Arthur Jeffery for kindly sharing his memories of the real life tragedy on Southampton Common which inspired this work of fiction.

ALI SPARKES

Ali Sparkes was a journalist and BBC broadcaster until she chucked in the safe job to go dangerously freelance and try her hand at writing comedy scripts. Her first venture was as a comedy columnist on *Woman's Hour* and later on *Home Truths*. Not long after, she discovered her real love was writing children's fiction.

Ali grew up adoring adventure stories about kids who mess about in the woods and still likes to mess about in the woods herself whenever possible. She lives with her husband and two sons in Southampton, England.

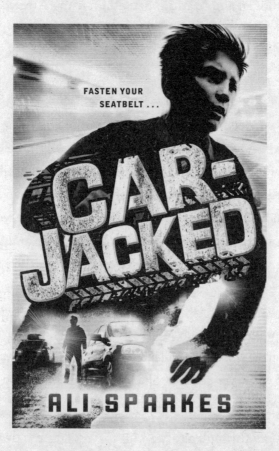

'Beethoven sucks,' said Jack.

Other kids might have sworn or shouted, 'I hate you!' Maybe kicked repeatedly at the back of the passenger seatin front. But this was much, much better. Genius, in fact. Because **a)** Mum loved Beethoven and **b)** Mum hated him using American slang.

Yes, it was perfect. The best way to create an explosion in the front seat. And it didn't fail.

'JACK!' Mum swung around, furious. Outside Dad carried on putting the fuel into the car. Jack could hear it squirting and gurgling down into the tank. 'Sometimes it's very hard to believe that you have an IQ of 170!'

Jack grinned at her. 'Mensa believes it!'

'Mensa never had to sit in a car with you while you talk like a four-year-old,' snapped Mum. Her face was pink and a little blue vein was throbbing in her right temple as she twisted further around to glare at him. 'For your information, Beethoven does *not* suck. For a start, that phrase has literally no meaning unless you're observing whether or not Beethoven is capable of drinking through a straw or inhaling through a tube. And given that he is dead, it's fair to say he can do neither. If, however, what you *mean* by "sucks" is that Beethoven is somehow *lacking* in any way, then I think we can perhaps remember that he is the most important classical composer of the eighteenth century—and was recognized as such when he was even younger than *you*.' She ended her short lecture with a tightly controlled exhalation.

Jack rolled his eyes and considered picking his nose. But Mum was ramping up enough already. It wasn't over yet.

'I would have thought,' she said, managing to speak entirely through gritted teeth, 'that you would have some kind of appreciation for Beethoven, as he too was a child prodigy.'

'Was he a child prodigy?' murmured Jack. 'Or just a child *podgy*?'

'That isn't even grammatically *correct!*' Mum took another deep breath and let it out slowly through her teeth, screwing up her eyes as if it hurt to look at him. 'WHY do you have to be SO loathsome whenever we take a holiday, Jack? Why?'

Outside, Dad put the petrol nozzle back into the pump with a clunk and screwed the fuel cap back on. He was whistling, trying to be jaunty, when he must know that all hell was breaking loose inside the Prius.

'Because I want a REAL holiday!' said Jack. 'You know—theme parks—tourist attractions—fast food!'

His mother looked as if he'd just said, 'You know — kicking puppies — setting fire to pensioners — hard drugs!'

She let out another long breath and struggled to keep control. 'Jack,' she said, using her *I am supremely calm* voice. 'We don't *do* tourism! We don't take you to tacky little attractions offering to deafen, maim or poison you! We take you to the real places. Mountains — forests — fossil-filled coastlines — wildfowl reserves. Other twelve-year-olds *might* get to ride the Fatal Nemesis Vampire of Oblivion at Walton Towers, but you — *you* get to see a *real eagle!*' Her voice became reverential. 'An *eagle*, Jack — in its *natural Scottish habitat!*'

Jack knew that seeing the eagle was a *huge* deal for Mum and Dad, but for him it had just been a blurry brown thing through the viewfinder of the binoculars. It hadn't really lived up to all the screaming and hyperventilating his parents had been doing. You'd think they'd been on the Vampire Nemesis themselves at that moment, instead of just bouncing slightly on a tartan rug on a hillside.

'Couldn't I just — for *once*,' he said, closing his eyes in the dramatic way his mother often did. 'Only *once* . . . have a McDonald's?'

There was a long silence. He opened his eyes and

found Mum looking at him as though she simply did not recognize him as her son any more. Her lips were compressed and her nostrils flared. Jack wondered whether he'd pushed her too far this time.

But honestly, what was the point of being one of the cleverest kids in Britain if you couldn't even score a cheeseburger out of it? Sadly, his mum and dad believed that McDonald's was the work of the Devil. Well, as good as. And eating a burger was much the same as slaughtering an infant over a chalk pentangle on the floor, while howling at the moon.

'It's just minced beef, Mum,' he muttered. 'Squashed into a round shape, fried and put in a bun with a bit of cheese on it. How much harm can it do me?!'

'If you don't understand the harm of giving in to fast food and becoming part of an international epidemic of obesity, then I just don't know *what* to say to you, Jack,' she concluded, turning back to face front and end their conversation.

'So—I guess a Mars Bar's out of the question too,' he said.

Mum screamed. Something quite rude. In Latin.

'If you're going to say things like that, perhaps you'd better find a language I *don't* understand,' he pointed out.

'If you keep this up,' she hissed. 'You can just *forget* the peat bogs!'

'Leonie!' Dad's shout from the petrol station shop distracted Jack from this horror (*Oh no—take anything from me—just not the trip to the peat bogs!*). 'My card won't work! I've forgotten my PIN again. Bring the other one will you?'

Mum grabbed her handbag and got out of the car, slamming the door behind her. Her angry stalk across the forecourt was ruined slightly when one boot-heel skidded on a puddle of oil, but she regained her poise within a second and was in the shop with Dad moments later. Through the shop window Jack could see a weary look on Dad's face which made his heart sink. He didn't want to ruin Dad's holiday.

He knew his little protest was pointless, anyway. Once Mum's mind was made up it was impossible to change. She had made up her mind, for instance, that Jack would be in college by the time he was fourteen. And as he'd already taken his first ten GCSEs—and passed them all with A*s—he guessed he would be. And then he would take around six A Levels in one year before zooming straight into Oxford or Cambridge by the time he turned fifteen. Mum couldn't *wait*.

So, while his cousins, Jason and Callum, were

hanging around the skate park and worrying about spots and girls and how to get a better score on Halo or Call of Duty or whatever they were into by then, *he* would be hanging around with eighteen-year-olds who wouldn't want anything to do with him. Not because he was deeply uncool (which, of course, he *was*) but because his MOTHER would be meeting him every day after lectures and making sure he wasn't sloping off for a junk food frenzy.

Jack groaned, lay down on the back seat and pulled the tartan car blanket over him from head to foot.

Ten seconds later the door opened and Dad thumped heavily into the driver seat, keyed the ignition at speed and shot out of the petrol station so fast that Jack was flattened into the upholstery in the rear.

Wow! Dad and Mum had had their rows before but this was obviously a bad one. As far as Jack could recall, Dad had never actually *abandoned* her before. He must have snapped.

He lay staring at the chinks of light in the blanket, wondering what to say to Dad. He felt a bit guilty. He had deliberately wound Mum up because he'd been fed up with her idea of a 'holiday'. . . but he didn't really mean for it all to go off like *this*. Dad sometimes lost it with Mum . . . but to leave her all alone at a petrol station in the middle of nowhere?

Jack knew he should say sorry. Tell Dad it was his fault; say he should go back. He would apologize to Mum and make it better.

He began to burrow out of the blanket and then froze. His first peek between the front seats showed a hand grasping the gearstick and wrenching it violently forward as the car veered around a tight bend on the narrow road, at breathtaking speed.

The hand was large and masculine. It had long lean fingers and blood smeared across its knuckles.

It was not his dad's.

HAVE YOU READ
THEM ALL?

THE SHAPESHIFTER

Ready for more incredible adventures? Try these!